I0719773

# WILLIAM RICHARDS

# STALKING P ART

*AS LONG AS YOU GET BACK UP, THERE IS ALWAYS A CHANCE TO SUCCEED.*

# PROLOGUE

BEING A MERCENARY IS DANGEROUS WORK. ALMOST all governments hate your guts, the Federation thinks you're a rogue or a menace, and, of course, there are more than a few bounties sitting over your head at any given time. In short, being the most renowned mercenary in the galaxy is a death wish. Well, for normal people at least.

My name is Rimor Dynex, and I'm the greatest merc this galaxy has ever seen. I've discovered more planets than you know to exist, I've rescued more races than you can count, and, most of all, I did it all while riding solo. Well, mostly.

Now that I'm retired from my work and my legacy in history is cemented, I've decided to take the time to share my stories. Not the watered-down tales in history books across the galaxy, but the real deal. So here we are. These are just a few stories from my days as a Merc. Buckle up.

# *PART 1*
## *A REGRETFUL ENDEAVOR*

"THIS IS RIDICULOUS. OUT OF ALL THE PLANETS on this side of the sea salt galaxy, I had to come to the last hunk of rock that's been charted in history. I don't even think this place has been charted by the feds. My pay better be worth it…"

I grumble the words while I run my hand through my hair, leaning back in my seat and staring up at the metal ceiling of my ship. 1,500 years of space travel and well over a thousand planets charted across the known universe—most of which had also been settled by one or two different species—and here I am travelling to the literal end of the galaxy.

And why, you might ask, would I take on such a cumbersome task? Two words: Calax Crystals.

Nothing special. You know, just one of the rarest—if not

*the* rarest—forms of crystal to ever be discovered in the galaxy. When they were first uncovered, few veins of the crystal existed, and finding them on planets with the resources already available to extract them safely was even more extraordinary.

Of course, let's say for the sake of argument I could just snag a few crystals on a more prominent planet. Well, that would bring up a slew of other problems—in particular, the not-so-small issue of Calax Crystals being outlawed by the SFF.

The SFF stands for Space Federation Force, but I like to refer to them as the pain in my ass...and with good reason. As the highest-ranking military throughout the galaxy—and in most respects a pseudo-government across worlds—they have authority to outlaw usage of such a material.

To me, they're nothing more than a bunch of fat cats sitting on their thrones, in the chambers of the planet Dubas, making meaningless decisions and calling them important. But that's a topic for another day.

Besides, in this one instance, the SFF might've had a decent reason for mandating such laws. See, Calax Crystals are this radical energy source that can leave a wake of destruction in its path if used inappropriately.

Unfortunately, those lessons had to be learned the hard way, and after the loss of thousands of lives from a mine explosion, they were unanimously outlawed as a source of power the next day. It's still the fastest law ever implemented.

So obviously, when I was approached about finding such a dangerous—not to mention illegal—crystal, I said no. Well, at least until I saw the paycheck. As a merc, when someone offers you enough money so that you could afford to buy a mansion on Dubas right alongside those fat cats, you don't pass that up. I guess what I'm saying is that every merc has a price—and mine is, apparently, about $500,000.

Now I'm sure you're also wondering who'd dare go around the backs of the SFF and request the collection of such an ultra-rare—not to mention stupidly dangerous—crystal?

Well, that request would come from a technologically savvy race known as the Bacardi. A bit of a strange looking group, even by my standards. They have the familiar shape of an earth human, but with eyes and fur on their body like a wily feline. Either way, they reside on a small group of planets in sector TB-12 known as The Indigo. The Bacardi are the furthest thing from a hostile race, and since they also like to stay within The Indigo and not explore any further, I've had more than enough business come my way, usually with similar payouts.

Strength might not be their best asset, but when it comes to technology, saying that they're advanced doesn't do it justice. Every great technological breakthrough in modern times feels like it comes out of The Indigo, and from the Bacardi specifically.

And if there's anybody that can attest to that technology, it's me. Without their work, I would've never been able to complete at least half of my missions, if not more.

See, one of the great assets that I have as a merc—besides a genius mind and finely honed instincts—is my one-of-a-kind space suit: the Dynex suit.

So if anybody could solve the mysterious powers of the Calax Crystals without blowing up their planet in the process, I don't think anyone — including the SFF — would doubt that the Bacardi could do it.

With all that in mind, and again because of the paycheck, I decided to take a crack at finding these crystals. Besides, if I failed, then no harm, no foul. I'd just be out far more fuel money than I cared to think about.

I doublecheck the planet's co-ordinates one last time. RG-87. This is my first visit to the outskirt planet and, with any luck, it'll also be my last. Going this far to the edge of the galaxy for a job would normally result in a huge hit in my profit margins, but with the massive amount of money to be earned, I'm swallowing my inner business acumen.

The Bacardi who'd asked me to go on this hunt had provided me with the planet's location, as it was uncharted at the time. But even when I received the co-ordinates, I had no clue it would be this far on the edge of the galaxy.

Aside from that, how their leader even knew Calax Crystals would be on an undiscovered planet was beyond me, but at the cost of losing my payday, I took him on good faith. Anyway, what was the worst that could happen?

I sit up in the cockpit of my spaceship (also designed by the Bacardi, for what it's worth) and stare at the never-ending vastness of space in front of me. Hanging in the black void sits a small planet that looks rather similar to the planet Dubas — well, at least from 400,000 kilometers away. The difference is, its large bodies of water have a heavy tinge of green, while Dubas has beautiful blue waters that I've always admired before landing.

A few twinkles of stars can be seen far off in the distance, and perhaps a moon is on the other side of the planet, but I have no intentions of finding out what counts as a full day here.

I click a few buttons on the dasher before flipping a switch. The large, curved, rectangular glass displays a series of holographic windows revealing a bevy of details about the planet's surface. Images of lush fields filled with green grass and tall blooming trees make RG-87 look far more beautiful than I expected. I guess that's what happens when the surface isn't cultivated for intelligent life by the SFF.

I chart my landing path, making sure I won't end up in some questionable area, but since there are no landing platforms or traffic control, I'm free to land pretty much anywhere I want.

With that in place, my ship begins its slow decent into RG-87's atmosphere. I still have some time before I land, so I head to the only other spot in my ship, or what I loosely call my closet space.

That's where I keep my prized possession—my Dynex suit. I walk up to the cylindrical canister in the middle of the room and tap a few buttons on the side panel, dropping the glass walls. There's nothing more beautiful in this galaxy than my Dynex suit after a fresh coat of polish. Takes my breath away every time. The perfect stone-green paint job mixed with gold accents on the shoulder guards, wrist components, and boots look quite sleek, if I do say so myself.

According to the group of Bacardi scientists who developed the suit, it'd been inspired by some famous scientist centuries ago who'd attempted to invent similar technology.

Currently, my suit resides on an exoskeleton in the canister so that none of the parts will get lost. To this day, the Bacardi haven't invented anything quite like my Dynex suit. The technology is so advanced and so powerful that the SFF outlawed any sort of mass production on the suit design, which also means that yours truly is the only known merc with the suit.

Others have tried to copy it through the years, and some have come close to creating knockoffs, but mine remains one of a kind.

Now, allow me to answer one simple question I'm sure you're wondering about: If the SFF outlawed the suit's production, how and why do I get to keep mine?

My friends, there's a simple reason for that. It's because I've come up through the ranks of the SFF. But those are days I like to avoid thinking about.

I tap the button on the center of the suit and watch it open, like someone cutting a human body right down the middle. I step in and let the machinery meld to my body like a wet suit. No matter how many times I've done it, the strange touch of metal latching onto parts of my skin always feels weird. On top of that, the sudden onset of blackness that comes with the helmet visor being turned off, and the momentary fear that my body is being molded and transformed without any power to stop it, always makes me hate getting in and out of the Dynex suit. That, however, is and always has been my only gripe when it comes to the technology.

Once I hear the snap of the latch on my back, I know I'm locked in, and I utter the magic words: "Link connect."

The pure darkness of the visor switches to covering my

vision in a tinge of blue. Some more data pops up in my peripheral vision, running a scan of the suit's mainframe and making sure everything is in working order. As expected, I get clearance and step back out of the canister, now in my full glory.

Before I'm set to go, I still need a few more supplies, or what I like to call the "mercenary essentials for stealth." Or, more appropriately, what the SFF declares legal for my profession. I pluck my plasma pistol off the hook on the wall beside me, and then grab my photon knife.

Much like for everything else, my suit has a special compartment for both of these weapons. On the back of the belt is a magnetic holster for my pistol, and on my left arm is a small compartment for my photon knife.

With a simple thought of what I desire, the compartment pops open on my wrist, and I place the silver rectangular hilt of the blade inside, making sure the clamps lock it in place. The two fit together like two puzzle pieces.

Once the compartment closes, I give my arm a quick shake, listening for any rattling. Few things in life scare a mercenary like faulty equipment, and that's a mistake I'll never make again. One time with a Vlad shark in the Seraph sea was enough.

Suited up and ready to go, I feel a pressure start to push down on me. I've hit the planet's atmosphere, and the gravity begins to take its toll. Luckily for me, my suit has a way of adjusting to different planets' pressures and atmospheres. Look, I'll admit that I don't understand every feature of this suit or how it all came to be, but I don't need to understand to be glad I have it.

The ship comes to a steady halt, and a green light from

the cockpit starts to flash, letting me know that the landing is a success.

Locked and loaded, I make my way back into the cockpit and take a peek out the windshield. After all, I only have pictures of RG-87 to go on and, as any merc would be, I'm curious about what a new planet might have in store. Boy, is *this* a mistake.

When I look out to the vast horizon of my next mission, I can't believe what I'm seeing. Either the pictures my ship have pulled up for me are dated by a few thousand years or I've landed on the trash part of the planet, because what I see is far from what I've been led to believe.

On my left sits a small lake of murky, greenish water, and I can only pray I won't be forced to swim in such disgusting gunk. Beside the lake, I've landed in a small clearing surrounded by rotting trees with wilted branches and lifeless leaves, if they even have any leaves left at all. I can even see signs of a vague, purple mist floating through the air. All in all, it looks more like a low-budget horror scene than the lush fields and sparkling water I was expecting.

"No wonder nobody's ever cultivated this planet," I mutter to myself, scanning my surroundings. "It's a shit hole."

I rub my visor, wondering if something is short circuiting. And then, for good measure, I pull up the pictures from before; I need to know that I'm in the right place. The coordinates match up, so I have to assume that I'm in the spot I should be. If nothing else, I can take a quick look around and be gone if the Bacardi informant had got his information wrong. Chances are I'll still be paid for my troubles, at least.

One last thing remains before I set off—I have to run an atmosphere test. For something so basic, you'd be shocked how many mercenaries I've met that forget to do this. Call it stupidity or call it arrogance—I don't know, but it's certainly not a way I'm intending to die.

A scanning probe on the front of my ship shoots out a long red laser, drawing in all the air particles needed to figure out the conditions. Once it does, my windshield monitor displays the report.

There's always a bunch of information that I don't understand or care about with these reports, but, thankfully, what I'm looking for shows up in bold letters at the top of my screen: "Oxygen levels - 0."

I read back the report and let out a groan. "Lovely. Well, good thing I came prepared, I guess."

Another one of the Dynex suit's great features is that it can hold more oxygen than most other space suits, and it doesn't require any bulk tanks on my back to do it, either. Instead, my oxygen supplies are kept in these small chemical tubes that are a modern-day wonder. Each tube is no longer than my middle finger, and they can hold up to eight hours of oxygen in them. Along with that, my suit regulates the oxygen with a slow release into my body, making sure all my levels stay where they should be.

As a precaution, I've brought four oxygen canisters, but since my suit can only hold three, that means I'll have a grand total of 24 hours on this mission, at least in one go-around. Not that I have any real concerns about being on RG-87 for so long—the goal is to do some exploring, with any luck find the Calax Crystals, and get out of here by dinner time.

That said, it's always good to be safe. I stuff the three canisters into an opening on my chest plate and let them sink into place.

"Good to go," I say to myself confidently, feeling the oxygen hitting my bloodstream. It always makes me feel a bit dizzy for a second or two. "Now let's see what this place has to offer."

When I walk down the metal ramp of my ship, the purple fog wraps itself around me. It didn't look this thick from the ship, but as I try to take in my surroundings, the density makes seeing things that much harder. What I can make out however, are lines of never-ending trees, most of which are dead or rotting.

I tap the right side of my helmet, and my visor switches from a blue tint to green. Of the never-ending list of features the Dynex suit has, my monster scanner will forever be the one that's made me so successful. Not only can it do a 200-foot scan for any lifeforms nearby—as long as they're producing heat—but if the lifeform had been discovered in the last 2,000 years, then my visor could trace the monster's origins, names, threat levels, and any other information that might be handy, all courtesy of the *Monster Hunter Encyclopedia*.

The *MHE* is a wonderful thing for any merc. Basically, it's a library for information on creatures from all over the galaxy. Oftentimes during a mission, information is a mercenary's best friend, which makes the *MHE* all the more useful. Added to that, I can run searches from anywhere in the galaxy, which means that on most days, I have more information with just a simple thought than most governments could dream of.

Scans now active, I take a full 360-degree look around my surroundings, allowing the visor to work its magic. However, to my surprise, no signs of life come up—only trees, water, and fog.

"Looks like the coast is clear. Now let's see what we're dealing with here."

As I start walking forward, I tap my left wrist and pull up a fully scaled-out 3D map of the area. That's also another by-product of my visor scan—it takes in my surrounding area and builds a map for me to use.

For the time being, it only shows me the small opening path in the forest, but as I explore further, I'll gather a much better lay of the land.

The third and final thing I need to do is run a check for Calax Crystals. After all, if they aren't even on this desolate piece of rock, then I'm just wasting my time.

However, I get lucky in this respect.

After meeting with the Bacardi about their request but before I'd left The Indigo, they provided me with a minuscule sample of Calax Crystals. Not enough that any research could come from it, but that wasn't the goal. As it turns out, Calax Crystals emit a distinct wavelength due to their chaotic nature, so with even the smallest sample, my suit can scan and detect them on any planet. Meaning that even though my map may be far from complete, small circles start to pop up in yellow. More than I would've thought, but that will make my job all the easier.

"Bingo—looks like we're in business. At least it wasn't a total waste of a trip," I muse, tapping my wrist to remove the map again. "Now I just need to get out of this forest first. Looks like I need to go a few miles north."

I start walking through the fog and it quickly envelops me. I take a quick peek behind me and realize I've already lost sight of my ship. The purple mist swallowed it up within seconds.

When I look back on this later, I'll likely think, "I should've known right then and there what I was getting myself into." But for now, I keep moving forward.

Each step through the crunchy dead grass below my feet brings me closer to my destination, but as it does, I know more dangers will approach. One look to my left, step, then another to my right and then a step again.

My scanners confirm no monsters are around, but that could change at any point, and I need to be ready, especially thanks to this mist coming off the ponds of water. On top of that, I was hopeful I might find some sign of civilization on this planet. I knew that odds were unlikely since it would have been reported previously, but this wouldn't be the first time I stumble upon a race that I shouldn't have.

No more than ten minutes into my travels, I can see the fog letting up. Also, the light's beginning to seep through and I know I'm getting close to the forest clearing.

But once I hit the edge of the trees, my surroundings don't get any better. Actually, in a weird way you could say they get worse. Like some mystical force, the mist stays bound to the forest as I leave, and with a clear view I see…nothing. Well, "nothing" might be misleading, but it's not totally inaccurate. What I do see is a grim and lifeless planet that stretches for miles with broken dirt like a desert, and not much else. To call it a barren wasteland would be an insult to wastelands all across the universe.

No, this place is a planet creeping up on the brink of death. The small patches of grass that do exist look like they've never seen water before, and the ground looks as frail and brittle as a rotted piece of wood. One wrong step and I could plummet to the middle of the planet, never to be seen again.

A first assumption might be that the planet is going through a severe drought. Then again, something about the planet's withering surface looks off—more like the planet's life is being drained itself, rather than a lack of refreshments.

But as a merc, none of that stuff matters to me. If RG-87 shrivels up and disappears into a black hole tomorrow, it would be of no concern to me. As long as I find the Calax Crystals and get my paycheck, at the end of the day, most everything else is irrelevant. Harsh as that may sound, it's the reality of the merc world.

I pull up my map again, and this time I can see where the Calax Crystals are much more clearly. From what I can make out based on the jagged shapes of the land and where the yellow dots are, my map suggests they reside near some sort of cliffside on the east end of a canyon. Only about fifteen minutes away.

At this rate, I assume this mission will be over fairly quickly.

Ready to make my way east, I hear a horrific screeching from above. Like a trained reflex—because it is—I reach around my back and grab my pistol, aiming it high into the sky. My finger remains on the trigger, ready and twitching.

The dull sun high in the sky starts to fade like a solar

eclipse, and then I'm absorbed by a massive shadow in the shape of a bird. I spin around to catch a glimpse of the red and black underbelly of the beast before it sails away, leaving me staring into the sun. I keep my gun at the ready, focused on the large vicious talons that protrude from the beast's feet. They're as long as my entire body, if not longer.

Before it can escape my view all together, I tap the right side of my helmet, and in my visor a small box forms around the beast's body. Keeping a steady eye, the white loading bar below the box shoots up to full. Once it does, more data on the beast is loaded before me:

---------------------------- **Dorneal: Bird Family, Female**

**Dorneals are known for their magnificent black fur and red crescent moon on their stomach. The fur allows dorneals to survive temperatures of minus 300 degrees Fahrenheit. Normally seen in packs traveling the skies for its next prey, the dorneal will use its sharp talons to rip its prey apart before ingesting food.**

**Threat Level: Three stars** -------------------------------------

A three-star threat is nothing to worry about, not for me anyway. I really only feel the need to concern myself with four- and five-star threats when it comes to creatures. That said, if I have no reason to mess with the dorneal, then I see no point in wasting either of our time.

Along with the information already on my visor, a few images of the dorneal also appear. I'm also shown a low-render 3D model of the creature, and then it shows me next to it for scale comparison. It's quite massive, even from high up in the air.

The beast continues to glide through the open skies, flapping its massive wings freely. Since it shows no interest in me, I drop my gun to my side. "Probably best to avoid that thing if at all possible."

Even with the dorneal gone, now that I'd caught a glimpse of the creatures roaming RG-87, caution needs to be taken.

My Dynex suit can survive the scorching temperatures of a plasma bullet or the freezing cold of a cryo chamber, but those talons on the dorneal look like they can cut through me like a hot knife through butter. Even as a fearless merc, sometimes it's just best to leave well enough alone.

To my surprise, the trip to the cliffside takes almost an hour. Perhaps my map isn't the most accurate in its time estimations.

Unfortunately, I have no way of speeding up my pace, but along the way I avoid making contact with any other creatures. There are still no signs of any intelligent life-forms either. Even so, my travels do eventually pay off in the form of a small beep sounding in my helmet. It beeps once every minute or so, but as I get closer to my desired target, it grows in steady increments. I'm getting close.

I come up along a stream of murky green water. I didn't know water could actually look dead, but this stream certainly does. All things considered though, water, whatever gross colour it is, must be a good sign.

The waterway leads me to the edge of a cliff, the same one I first pinpointed as my target. I walk around the edge of the cliffside looking for any sort of path downward, but I instead eventually come to a small lifeless waterfall. It's all but dried up, a lackluster stream pouring out of its mouth onto a pile of jagged rocks below. A fall from this far would be a certain and painful death.

However, the lack of a stream gives me a great view of the cave hidden beneath the waterfall's mouth about half-way down. I use my visor to zoom in as far as it can go. Barely through the faded murky waters, I can see a white outline along the wall. It's in no discernible shape, which means that if my hunch is correct, the Calax Crystals are scattered throughout the cave. Well, either that or they're deep within the walls, in which case I'd need to find a way to drill through them. This is one of the rare things my Dynex suit can't do—but regardless, one way or another I'll be getting my hands on those crystals.

With that determination firmly nestled in my mind, I still have one small issue. There's no simple path to my destination. After a quick estimation, I'd say the drop is somewhere between 500 and 600 feet, with nowhere to land in between.

I have thrusters that I could use to slow any rapid descents, but, as handy as they are, they also have limitations to their strength, and at best will keep me from dying on a 100-foot drop. Nothing more. Even adding in my shock absorption from the suit, a leap down would end with my legs jammed through my skull. And that's putting it mildly.

I try to wrack my brain around what the best course of action is, but little do I know that my decision is about to be made for me.

A not-so-distant screech, kind of a mix between a falcon and dinosaur, pierces my ears like a sharp cry. I've heard this cry before, though—not too long ago, actually. My gun drawn and at the ready, I leap away from the cliff and turn, only to see a dorneal, most likely the same one from before, divebombing me. A hungry look takes over its eyes, and it seems that I appear to be the main course for the day.

I fire off three shots, but each blast singes into the bird's thick fur with little effect. The beast keeps its course and points its long talons at me, shooting toward my chest like an arrow. With only fractions of a second to spare, I roll out of the way. The dorneal comes crashing down with its talon ripping through the brittle ground with ease. Before it can turn and smack me with its massive wings, I jump in the air, using my thrusters to keep my height for a few seconds.

"Well, if I can't damage your fur, at least I can take out your sight."

Two pinpoint shots connect with the dorneal's blood red eyes as I fall back to the ground.

It screams as green streaks of what I assume is blood drip from the monster's cavernous eye holes. The next scream, this one more of a grumbling roar, indicates that my plan has worked. It rips its talons out of the ground and begins flailing about blindly, swinging its wings at me.

Whether it's an act of desperation or a plan to send me off the cliff, the bird's wild behaviour gives me the opportunity I need to strike.

Thanks to the dorneal's massive wingspan, each time it

swipes, it creates a gust of air acting as an updraft. That's my new plan. I jump again and, using a combination of my thrusters and the updraft, I soar higher and toward the blind monster. I zoom past its head, narrowly missing the beak by inches, and then grab a thick tuft of fur on its back and swing my way around to the nape of its neck. It flails wildly and tries to shake me off like a flea, but I hold on with a death grip and continue climbing up my new pet's back.

Without strong knowledge of the dorneal nerve system, I—as the surgeon—am doing a little bit of guess work, but once I finish climbing to the top of the neck, I pinpoint my mark.

Still hanging on with one hand while the dorneal does all it can to shake me loose, I hold my left arm parallel to it. Like a switchblade being flipped out, my photon knife jets out from the top of my wrist. The searing of my knife sounds like hot metal being submerged in water.

Normally, my photon knife (and one that any other mercenary carried) wouldn't be nearly strong enough to cut through fur this thick—at least if my blaster pistol does nothing, I safely assume—but the reason I keep it in a compartment in my suit is because of its added power. When in the Dynex suit, calling it a knife is quite inaccurate; it's far closer to the size and strength of a short sword.

I slip my knife into the beast's neck, letting it seep in an inch further at a time. I want to tame the bird and render it unconscious—that's the best-case scenario. Frankly, I have no desire to kill the blasted thing. It serves me no purpose, and killing creatures on foreign planets tend to have lasting effects that I and everyone else have no way of predicting. It could cause problems for years to come.

However, with what happens next, I wish I had.

Instead of the beast collapsing on the ground from pain, or even just wearing itself out from its flailing like I anticipate, it takes off like a jet, high into the sky.

*Damn thing…why won't you just lay down?* I feverishly grumble, trying to predict its movements. It's like a wild animal being backed into a corner.

The bird was leaving me no other choice. Like I said earlier, killing creatures on foreign planets isn't something I like to do, and I definitely won't go out of my way to shed more blood then necessary, but that doesn't mean I won't. Survival of the smartest.

My knife already planted into the bird's neck, I pull it out and start stabbing repeatedly.

The dorneal bends its neck down while shrieking in pain, giving me an accurate look at how high up I am. And it's not good. The ground looks like nothing more than a distant brown sea, which means I'm much higher than I first realized.

Whatever this oversized pigeon's plans are, I'm not about to waste time figuring them out. I keep stabbing with my left arm while hanging on with my right. Three vicious stabs later, I guess I finally hit some sort of nerve system based on the unholy roars of agony that seemed to reach into the far depths of space. The struggle to shake me loose ceases, and the dorneal's frenetic flapping comes to a complete stop. Like a rocket running out of steam, the bird begins to float in the sky for a moment before turning over and making its sharp decent, and taking me with it.

I don't know what terminal velocity is in the Dynex suit, but this is the closest I've ever come to finding out.

Firing toward the surface like a meteor, I hang on with a death grip praying I won't rip the fur off of my ride. It appears that I'd been flown straight up, because as we plummet back to the planet's surface, I can see the lifeless waterfall come into sight. That's when I'm struck with a brilliant plan. My grip already tight enough to rip the dorneal's fur out, I try to shift its body weight by leaning into my own. I'll admit it's not the most effective strategy in the world, but when you're soaring to your final doom on the back of a giant, dead bird from thousands of feet up, you do what you can.

"Just a little further, you ridiculous behemoth…you got me into this mess, and now you're gonna get me out of it," I seethe through gritted teeth. I say some other choice words too, but they're better left not repeated here.

Our speed continues to accelerate, and the cliffs become much clearer to see. If I'm to pull this off, I need to time my jump to perfection. And, even at best, that'll only *lower* my risk of death, not negate it. I pass into the opening gap of the cliffs and right toward the jagged rocks at the bottom. This is my cue. I release my death grip and jump toward the inner walls. Below me, the lifeless husk of the dorneal crashes into the jagged rocks, not only leaving it in a bloody mess but probably causing a small earthquake as well.

I, on the other hand, shoot out my photon sword and jam it into the side of the cliff, slicing through the brittle rock as I sail down.

If there was one thing I failed to consider with my plan, it's the frail state of the planet. My sword is sharp, of course it is, but at the rate it's slicing through the cliff, my speed's not slowing down nearly enough to save my skin.

Sparks shoot off in all directions, but my rapid decent refuses to halt. No amount of shock absorption will save my bones from shattering. I start to assess my options, though they're beginning to run out.

I still have one final hope, though. My thrusters. I activate them, feeling the jarring shock on my body as my momentum breaks considerably. My head wants to go through the top of my helmet, and my teeth feel like they're a bite away from shattering.

Combining my sword and thrusters, though painful on the body, gives me the best chance to live, so now all I can do is trust in my plan. And also pray like hell.

With only a marginal improvement to my survival, I look down. Seeing the dorneal and the rocks, I figure I have about eight seconds or so until impact. Knowing that's of little use, I push the internal timer out of my head and fix my gaze on the bird below me.

*This is my chance.* In one swift motion, I rip my sword from the rock wall and leap toward the husk laying on the ground.

Since slowing my momentum has run its course, I need to look for the next best option. Which, as it turns out, is landing on the softest surface possible to cushion the blow. That leaves me between a rock and a dorneal. I choose the dorneal. I catch just enough of the wing to absorb some impact, but with almost no resistance from the dead creature I push the wing into the stomach of the beast, crashing into it with a bone rattling thud.

Turns out, dorneal fur isn't so soft when you crash into it at a blazing speed. Still, it's better than bedrock.

I roll off its stomach and land face down on the dirt, my eyes closed and my heart pounding through my suit.

"Am I alive…?" I groan, lifting my head up just enough to look forward. Small pebbles continue tumbling in around me from the damage I caused, but other than that, I and everything around me seem to have survived the detour. All except for the dorneal.

I get to my knees, which is all I can manage for the moment, and look back at the giant bird. I know it's dead. Blood drips down it eyes and neck, jagged rocks pierce its right wing, and its large feet sport broken talons, but, even so, every mercenary has a level of paranoia built into them.

No words would be able to describe my fear and anger if, by some miraculous will of God, this damn bird that caused all of this had lived.

On top of all that, I can still feel my internal organs rattling around like a box of loose toys. I have no energy for another fight with this demonic wretch.

Now, with that being said, I do—for just a brief moment—feel a tinge of sadness in my heart. I know RG-87 appears on the surface to be a dying planet of sorts, but all creatures in the universe have a family somewhere. We often forget that aspect of things, and it's especially poignant since the SFF continues to wipe out more and more species. Year upon year, we can see the impact we have on wildlife getting worse.

Also, every planet has an intricate ecosystem that's been developed and maintained over thousands of years, and removing any part of that system can cause irreversible damage. I know for a fact that I am one of the only mercs that actually follows that philosophy, as most will just kill anything they deem hostile at first glance. After all, the lingering effects will more than likely never be noticed until my generation is long gone. Still, I feel it's my moral duty to recognize my part in things.

Even with all of that consciously on my mind through each mission, the life of a mercenary is hardly a peaceful one. You grow accustomed to the bloodshed, as strange as that sounds. And trust me—you grow used to it quicker than I'd care to admit.

Although, this beast *did* want my head as a trophy for its talons, so I dust myself off with a clear conscience and get ready to move on. I still have a mission to complete.

My first step is to check my suit for any malfunctions from the fall. But there's seemingly no need for damage reports—hardly a scratch on it—and it's obvious that a suit of metal is way more durable than some mercenary.

After a quick scan, the beeping starts up once again, this time much louder and quicker. I'm close, and with nothing standing between me and the Calax Crystals now, I can see my goal in sight.

Even better, I landed only a few feet away from the hollowed-out entrance of the cave. I can still see the white silhouette representing the previously elusive objects of my desire, only this time much clearer.

I make my way behind the dripping waterfall and into the cave, and all I can see is the white shroud of what I'm after deep in the distance.

The further in I explore, the more the light fades and my visor switches to night vision mode. This gives me a much better view of my surroundings. I catch faint twinkles, like stars in the night sky, in the distance of the cave.

I get closer, and the stars start to sparkle all around me. Around the walls are sharp, white crystals protruding out in all sorts of directions, with dozens of large veins pulsating into them. They're rather tiny compared to what I'd imaged, only being about the size of my oxygen canisters, but that makes them all the easier for me to store.

Except one problem remains: I'd only expected to find a few crystals at best. But there must be enough in this cave to make ten times my commission if I decide to sell this stuff on the black market instead. Too bad they're such a pain to reach.

I walk up to the nearest clump of crystals and stick my hand out. Even through my suit, I can feel the extreme heat radiating off them, and it warms my fingers like a glove. It has the same feel as the small sample I'd been given by the Bacardi, but just to confirm I'm looking at the right stuff, I run a quick scan.

------------------------ **Calax Crystal: Material, Crystallite**

**One of the rarest sources of energy in the known galaxy. Calax Crystals are formed through hundreds of years of extreme shifting temperatures in a planet's core. Preliminary studies of the crystal show only a few handfuls can provide enough energy to power some small worlds for close to a decade. However, due to the chaotic nature of the energy source, they have been formally banned by the Space Federation Forces as part of Clause 122 Subsection 3 of the SFF Rights and Safety Act.**

**Threat Level: Five stars** -------------------------------------------

I try to ignore the last line of my scanner's information. I already know I'm in a bit of a moral grey area with this mission. But here's how I see it: I might be the one collecting illegal crystals and shipping them to a planet, but I'm not the one *using* them. And if you read the technicalities of the law — and I have — I'm not breaking the Safety Act. I doubt any government or court of law would look at my actions in the same way, but I can spare some money on bail anyways with this kind of a payday.

I activate my photon knife and tap the base of the crystal like I'm cutting the stem of a flower. I need to move with caution. Based on my limited knowledge, the crystals don't react with each other, which means that chipping away chunks of them won't be too dangerous, but knowing the reactive properties of such power, I have no interest in blowing myself up — not to mention the cave and probably the whole planet with one false move.

For looking as solid and dense as regular crystals, cutting through the base proves surprisingly easy. I let the heat of my blade do the work, continuing to inch forward until I reach the end and feel the clump fall into my hand. From there, I cut them up into even smaller pieces so they're more manageable to carry.

If my suit does have a downside, I can say with confidence that it's the lack of storage space. The Dynex suit has been optimized to the point of mindboggling efficiency. Everything you can imagine has a specific space made only for its sole purpose. Take my photon knife — there's no space for anything else in its compartment. It fits my knife and nothing else. Also, the only free compartment I have is in a rather awkward spot, under my armpit stretching a third of the way down my forearm. Thanks to the sheet of metal wrapped around my arm on the inside of the suit, I have no way of feeling the crystals being log jammed under my arm, but still, whenever I use that compartment, it always feels like something is slivering up and down my limb.

I counted 13 pieces in total, which is a fair bit more than had been originally asked for. But hell, if I'm going to go through all this trouble for such powerful gems, then I might as well take a souvenir or two for myself.

With item in tow and my mission halfway over, all that's left to do is make a return trip to my spaceship. Preferably without another dorneal (or something worse) attempting to make me its snack.

After I exit the cave, I take a look at my oxygen supply. Twenty hours left.

"Well, that took longer than I'd planned. But beggars can't be choosers I suppose."

With such a high safety margin of oxygen left, I have nothing to worry about. However, scaling the side of this cliff will be a pain in the ass. Lucky for me, the damage I created on my expedition downward gives me a decent number of ledges to help me climb back up. It'll still take some effort, but with my sword and thrusters intact, I can manage.

The scorching heat of what feels like two entire suns beats down on me as I climb up the side of the cliffs. I know it has to be bad, because my suit acclimatizes quite well to all temperatures. For me to feel any sort of discomfort means that it's becoming hellishly hot.

After almost another hour of climbing, I reach my hand

up and grab the cliff's final ledge. I toss my left leg over first and then my right before rolling over and sprawling out on my back, looking up at the grim, grey sky.

I take a deep breath and sit up.

"If I never see this rock again it will be too soon," I huff.

As a merc, you try to keep yourself in great shape. If you don't, you'll die quick—believe me. I've seen it. But that being said, climbing those cliffs takes a lot of stamina out of me, and the heat sure doesn't help, either. But by the time I reach the top, I'm ready to return to my ship and get a little shuteye while I hurl through space back to The Indigo.

Another hour of oxygen disappears as I walk back to the forest, and even in that short time my surroundings look different than my memory recalls. The trees are withered even more than previously, with the bark peeling off like banana peels and the brittle dirt looking like ash. The sun must be drying out all the life on this planet.

Along the way, I see another point of interest. A bit to the west of the forest's entrance, I spot a section of strange-looking bikes. I raise an eyebrow wondering if there indeed is intelligent life on this planet. Or, God forbid, the SFF.

Worried that the SFF will see my spaceship, I hurry back through the forest. I know they have tabs on my ship, and the last thing I need is some sort of investigation.

Then I hear the sharp sound of a branch as it snaps in half, only it wasn't caused by my running. My instincts propel me to dart behind the thickest tree I can find and conceal myself. The purple fog has returned, which will play into my stealth efforts this time.

With my eyes darting back and forth, I look for any sort of lifeforms. To my left, I catch a glimpse of a red and black silhouette of some kind, but I can't tell if it's human before the fog swallows it up. From what I can tell, it does have a somewhat human body-like shape, but through the fog, even the heat maps are wavering.

That said, it seems like a safe assumption it isn't some random indigenous creature snooping around.

Based on the way it moves, it mirrors a human's walking motions, or some other lifeform with similar movements. The body is also much bulkier. But perhaps it's just space armour. However, there's no chance I'm risking getting too close until I figure out who's occupying this desolate planet. Not while I'm carrying illegal goods, at least.

If humans or some other race of intelligence live here, then I need to be cautious, and even more so if it's the SFF. Yes, the goods are concealed away in my suit, but what the naked eye fails to see, technology will always detect. Especially in the case of the SFF.

From firsthand experience, I'm well aware of their protocols. They can run a scan on my body in seconds and find if something is amiss. Then I'll be forced to either comply and deal with the consequences or attempt to make a run for it and see how badly that turns out. I care for neither option at the moment.

Giving myself adequate time to make sure nobody is sneaking up on me, I start my pursuit.

Each calculated step through the dead trees and misty fog ensure I avoid any branch or leaves that can potentially sound the alarm of my presence.

Inch by inch I approach, until a faint glimpse of a red

and black silhouette appears in my visor again. I'm getting close. First I see one, then a second, and soon I realize that a full swarm of 12 beings are nearby. I take a peek through the tree, my hand resting on my gun. Off in the distance and only a couple dozen feet away sits my spaceship, just where I'd landed it.

Unfortunately, this confirms the one scenario I'm most afraid of. It seems obvious that whoever this group is, they're searching for my ship. I say this because as far as I can tell, the forest holds nothing else of value in its decrepit state.

In the back of my mind, I have a glimmer of hope that, if granted an opening, I can make my escape undetected. Doing so would allow me to take off, and from there I'll just have to find a place to lay low.

Except that finding my spaceship turns out to only be the beginning of my problems.

The most obvious thing I can see is that the door to my ship is missing. Or, more aptly, it's been ripped off and tossed aside like a broken cabinet door. Whatever these things are, they clearly don't care for other people's belongings.

Are they scavenging my ship for parts? I know of some species with the power to disassemble pretty much any hunk of metal they find and sell it for profit, but for whatever reason, this seems unlikely.

I wonder if they're searching for something specific inside. Considering what's in there, I'm not too worried. There isn't much of note—maybe an old sandwich or some clothes—and with me being in possession of my gun, knife, and Dynex suit, they can take any of the other things and I'll still be fine.

Or perhaps they're a less-advanced spices and are marvelling at the technology of ship, trying to study it. That would be the best-case scenario, but also the least likely by far, I figure.

I take another few steps forward, inching as close as I can. With the gap narrowed down to a few feet, I can start to make out some of the features on these lifeforms. Although not distinct, I can spot sharp, scythe-like hands that have a deep-mooning arc, and strange almost prehistoric looking heads.

My heart skips a beat, as another similar image flashes onto my visor. I scurry to the next tree and get close enough for it to achieve a clear scan. What pops up sends chills down my spine. It's certainly the last thing I'm expecting to see on this planet, and something I'd hoped to never see again.

------------------------- Uuzik: Lifeform, Dinosaur family

**Uuzik, or Uuziks, are an intelligent species that derives from creatures known as dinosaurs that lived in southern parts of the galaxy. Over thousands of years, these dinosaurs developed and evolved until around the year 2,400, when they would become known as the Uuzik species. They are a hostile race and should be avoided. If spotted, contact the SFF right away.**

**Threat Level: Four stars** -------------------------------------------

The text scrolls up like credits at the end of a movie.

Reading that simple description on my visor did nothing to detail the horrors that truly encompass the Uuziks. Allow me to give you some tidbits of information here.

The Uuziks are much like the description on my visor. A developed race from dinosaurs, but far more intelligent. They started off as a poor race of bandits that fed off space drifters, but as time went on, they started to radicalize, developing more cunning and torturous plans. Nowadays, they're known for causing numerous genocides of smaller planets, along with enslaving various races, stealing resources of planets, and, in some cases, capturing and selling entire planets to other war lords of similar ilk. As far as hostility goes, no race in the galaxy is as cutthroat, which is why the SFF has been at war with them for decades now, but with little success to show for it.

I can feel deep pits of sweat bleeding through my clothes and pooling up in the bottom of my suit. I can't believe my luck. I don't *want* to believe it. If there is a god, clearly it's decided that today would be my day of punishment. *I guess that's what I get for trying to smuggle Calax Crystals. Christ.*

When I get a second look at the monstrosities that are the Uuziks, I know my scanners are right. Because, well, *of course* they are. They always are.

More Uuziks continue to appear from behind my ship, circling it and tapping around on the outside.

Let me tell you: Seeing the vilest, most monstrous lifeforms known in the galaxy circling my only way off a believed-to-be deserted planet is one hell of a sinking feeling. Even worse than that, they're standing between me and my freedom from RG-87, or, more bluntly, the biggest payday I might ever receive in my career.

Of course, this will be far from the last time I have to deal with these vicious monsters, but today marks the first time I've seen a group of Uuziks in many years.

Uuziks come in many shapes and sizes, and over the years I'm pretty sure I've seen them all, but these ones are actually smaller than usual. They're about my height, though they carry much more weight to them. The Uuziks' bodies look like plated armour that's been stitched together with a red and black bare breastplate, while the rest of the body is a mossy green colour.

They stalk around my ship with a hunch in their backs, their legs a fair bit shorter than their bodies. To top things off, they have these prehistoric heads with bones that look like their own spaceship wings sticking out of them.

On more than one occasion, I've seen these bastards snap someone's neck with ease. I have no interest in being their next target.

Once I get a grip on my new reality, many different scenarios and issues run through my head.

The first problem is numbers — as in the number of *them*. They have a lot, and I have…me. Perhaps if there was only one Uuzik or two…maybe even three, then I could've either attempted to scare them off or even bully my way through in a one-versus-three duel, but not this many. I count 12 or possibly 13 of them, though when they walk behind my ship, I lose count. The point is that I'd be overrun and killed within seconds of revealing myself.

When you become a mercenary, it's all but written in the job description that you'll be dealing with unsavory groups. It's not always ideal, and you need to be on your toes at all times, but if you want work, well…it is what it is.

That being said, if there's any one race I have no interest in dealing with on any level, it's the Uuziks. They're a race built solely on power and tyranny. When it comes to their interactions with others…well, they have a simple motto, which in their native tongue translates to, "spare no lives." A motto I know they take to heart.

By this time, I've done hundreds of missions ranging from large to small, but not a single one required me to deal with the Uuzik race. I've made sure of that, and with good reason.

The first time I came into contact with an Uuzik was as an infant. To call it an unpleasant experience would be a vast understatement. It was 25 years ago when the Uuziks first arrived on my home planet of Earth. We as a species were one of the oldest and most developed planets in the way of technology at the time, and over the planet's history, many different races had come and gone, admiring not only our technology but also the beauty of our planet for its lush nature and industrialized advancements. Some other races had even moved to the planet permanently, bringing their own technology with them so that we could advance our civilization further. Not that I ever got to see those days. In the end, such prosperous life would only serve to make Earth a bigger target.

Up to this point, the Uuziks were well known for smaller crimes, attacking on unsuspecting prey with brutal war-crime-like precision, but they had yet to attempt a full-scale take-over of a first-rate planet. They wanted to send a message to the SFF, and, for whatever reason, they deemed Earth to be the most suitable target to start with.

Honestly, I don't remember much about that day, or

even most days that followed. But what I do remember I've tried to bury in the farthest depths of my mind, never to be thought of again.

The Uuziks might be known for selling planets to war lords, but selling a perfectly functioning livable planet is far from the Uuzik way. In Earth's case, first they proceeded to drain all of the planet's natural water. Then they moved on to its other abundance of resources. Of course, that was only after geocoding an estimated 96% of the planet's life-forms, most of which were part of the human race. My race.

I honestly don't know how I survived the onslaught, and in reality, I probably shouldn't have. All I remember is my parents attempting to hide me from the monsters, and then everything going black. When I woke, my parents and anybody else from my small town were missing. All of them were accurately presumed dead.

One could say that I was spared, but that was being far too optimistic of the Uuziks. My perspective—and this still seems the most likely—is that I survived off the back of dumb luck. Nothing more and nothing less.

I can't tell you how long I remained on Earth after that fateful day. A day I guess, maybe two, but there's no way a baby of my age could survive much longer than that. One thing I do know for sure is that the Federation wasted no time sending waves of troops to dock on Earth and stop the Uuziks. However, as is the Federation's way, they took their sweet time coming to the rescue of my people. By the time they finally decided to pull the trigger and help, the Uuzik surprise attack had already been successful and the planet was left in shambles.

I will give them a sliver of credit, though, for saving

any of the remaining life on earth once they arrived. They took all the survivors and helped them start new lives on refugee planets across the galaxy.

Well, all but one of them. I was the unfortunate winner of what I call the "Federation Sweepstakes." In other words, I was granted no such opportunity to refugee on a new planet.

Not that those who lost everything were living some grand, amazing new life; no, not by any means. They were on a backwater planet scraping to survive under the Federation's protection. But even *that* was better than the cards fate had dealt me.

While I call it a "Sweepstakes," the winner had actually been picked from the beginning. For whatever reason, the Federation had decided that I would be staying with them. Obviously, I wasn't given a say in this matter as I was no more than an infant, and to this day I still haven't been given a proper reason as to the Federation's logic on the subject. At this point I doubt I ever will, but I guess it doesn't matter now.

After the fall of Earth, and for the first 18 years of my life, I was locked under the Federation's thumb. I might have only been a child, but when it comes to those bastards there's no such thing as a childhood. I spent countless hours between physical and mental training until I could become a full-fledged SFF solider.

And let me tell you, I hated every second of those days. The grueling workouts that made me vomit, the never-ending tests and quizzes about political law, all the way down to the stuffy uniforms. Oh—and the complete desensitization to traumatic events. Right, that's a big one, too.

The only thing I *am* grateful for is how it contributed to my broader goal, which was steeped in revenge on the Uuziks. But as I grew older and continually saw the horrors committed by the monstrous race, I grew weary of getting involved in such a dangerous—if not outright stupid—fight. If I could avoid it, I had no interest in dying at the hands—or more specifically, the claws—of those who wiped out the majority of my race.

But back to the present moment. Convinced my situation couldn't get any worse, I suddenly see this...this *thing* almost twice the size of a normal Uuzik stomp out of my ship. It resembles the other Uuziks, but it has the demeanor of something you'd find in a child's nightmare. No doubt it isn't a natural evolution of the Uuzik birth line, but some sort of mutant among mutants. It's bathed in the same colours as normal Uuzik skin, but the colours look faded compared to its brethren. Scales crawl up its back like roof shingles and all the way down to the long, winding tail that drags behind it.

The beast steps out of my ship and down the small ramp. For good measure, he slams his tail behind him, smashing my ramp into pieces. I clench my fist and remain quiet, not because I'm seeking retribution, but because of the damage. *That ramp was damn expensive...*

The monster turns away from my ship and looks into the forest. In my direction. I don't know how long he holds his gaze for, because I'm too busy hiding behind the trees and silently reciting every prayer I can think of.

I listen intently for any sound of footsteps heading my way, but they never come.

After a few seconds, I have to take a peek. Once I do, I catch a clean glimpse of the beast, and my memories come flooding back.

I've come into contact with this thing before—this exact one—on that fateful day while I still lived on Earth. This Uuzik was the portrayed leader of the race. The king, and the strongest and most ruthless among them. He'd arrived in my city that day, and he was the one who roamed through the streets killing all who stood in his way. How many people did he kill that day…hundreds? No, probably *thousands* of innocent lives.

Until now, I'd forgotten his face, but with my memory awakened I know I need to leave. And whether that's via my spaceship or some other means, it doesn't matter; I just need off this planet. My blood is boiling with that same anger I've held onto since I was a kid, but now isn't the time for revenge.

I take a deep breath and compose myself. If there was even a sole chance that I could take on a hoard of Uuziks surrounding my ship and attempt an escape, it went up in smoke with this monster's arrival.

Maybe I can create a diversion and draw the Uuziks away from my ship, but after a quick calculation on the engines' start-up time, not to mention the noise it would make taking off, they'd no doubt catch me. And even if they didn't stop me from making it to space, there's no way they'd dare let me go freely. They'd begin hunting me through space, making sure I can't alert the SFF.

And since I'm already trying to smuggle Calax Crystals back to The Indigo, contacting the SFF for help would be just as much of a death wish.

With no other choice, I choose to stay hidden and just pray that they don't ransack my ship too badly.

Waiting for them to finish searching my ship feels endless. At some point, even more Uuziks arrive, adding to my angst and fear. Yeah, I'll admit it—by this point, I'm a bit terrified. Especially because these ones come wielding machines the likes of which I've never seen. They are long metal rods, like crow bars, but glow red in the middle. Every square inch of my ship, both inside and out, are being examined with these machines, down to the last roof tile. Yet from what I can gather, nothing's been taken. None of the technology, none of the parts, not even the snacks I left in the back…something is off here.

Are they looking for something specific aboard my ship? If so, I don't know what it could possibly be, but why else would they take so long and leave everything intact? Either way, I figure I should be thankful for the lucky break and not question it. Now if they'd just leave, maybe I can make my escape and forget this day ever happened. After I get paid, at least.

In reality, the entire ordeal takes less than an hour, but while you're sitting behind a tree watching your ship being stalked about, that hour can feel like an eternity.

Finally, I hear a low series of grumbles coming from the leader of the Uuziks as he points toward my ship and then points back to the path down the forest. I have no clue what they're saying and I'm not close enough for my visor to provide a translation, but from what I can gather based on their gestures, they're gearing up to leave. Thank Christ.

I take this opportunity to sink a little further back into

the misty forest, ensuring I won't blow my position. Not after holding out for this long.

But as it turns out, what I'd believed to be an order to evacuate the area and head back from whence they came ends up being something far worse.

A couple of Uuziks start tapping my ship with their claws, placing small hockey puck-shaped circles on it. *Are they tagging my ship so that I'll be tracked through space? Does this mean they'll be waiting for me to get into the air and then try to shoot me down?*

Admittedly, even though I've always had great skills as a merc, if there's an area in which I fall short, it's being a great pilot. I actually hate flying. To this day, I absolutely loathe it. It's so eerie floating through an endless darkness, knowing that from any angle I could be shot at or hit by an asteroid. Even with all the technology of the modern era making travel safer, it still always put me on edge.

I come to a simple realization: If I'm to escape successfully, I need to understand their plan better.

After falling back into hiding, I change my course and start to creep closer than anyone would consider safe. I only need to get within a close enough distance so that their voices can be picked up clearly. This would be a lot easier without all the trees around, reflecting the sounds and distortions. But then again, without the trees, I'd be dead anyways.

Even though they speak a strange foreign dialect, my suit can, naturally, provide a rough translation for me.

With every inch forward, the low rumbling grumbles of the monsters slowly become clearer. I take a knee in the bushes and let my suit do the rest.

In a male robotic voice generated by my visor, I start to hear English speaking voices.

"Boss, we've searched the outside of the ship and the rest of the inside, but there's nothing more than a few useless knickknacks. Our men have foot soldiers from base searching beyond the forest, but still no signs of the pilots yet. They couldn't have got far, though. We'll find them."

This conversation is taking place between the Uuzik boss and one of his subordinates. The massive oversized Uuzik takes a brief look around, and for a second he stops. His beady eyes stare directly into my path.

I freeze. Can he see me? There's no way. I'm hidden behind more shrubs, trees, and fog then are even necessary. I call the leaders bluff and remain still, trusting my judgment. This time, I'm rewarded when the leader Uuzik turns back to his underling and begins speaking. Unfortunately, that'll be the last of my breaks for now.

"I refuse to take a single chance that this is some wandering passerby," the tyrant says. "It could be an operative Federation dog sent here in an unmarked ship. See to it that any foul dogs are stomped out before they can escape. If it's a Fed, kill them immediately. Do not let them get anywhere near the facility."

Even with the loose translation, the intended tone of his voice comes in loud and clear. This guy isn't playing around.

"What do we do about the ship?" the lackey asks.

"Dispose of it. We don't want our little dog making a return trip to space behind our backs."

*Dispose of it? Shit.*

This is when the panic really sets it. My heart starts pounding so loud I'm convinced it'll give away my position. And the cold sweats running through my body might actually short circuit my suit. I need to act, and quick. But there are still far too many of the Uuziks to deal with.

I'm left with a conundrum no merc wants to face. Two options, each with an unappealing result: I can either die to a bunch of Uuziks, or I can die stranded on RG-87.

Although neither is ideal, I keep a cool head about me and decide on the latter. If I rush headlong in, I'll be killed within seconds. Quick, but definitely painful. On the other hand, if I wait things out, I'll be giving myself more time to think of a more successful plan.

As much as I hate the thought of exercising patience, I need to play the long game here. So instead, I'm left to watch in agony as, one by one, the Uuziks finish wiring my ship with more hockey pucks and start to march out to the entrance of the forest. All of them, that is, except for the leader. It's like he knows I'm waiting for him to leave—he sticks around looking in my direction and then back at my ship. He's waiting me out and seeing how I'll react, and we both know it.

I can hear the beeping in the background start to quicken as the final Uuzik leaves. Now I understand why the leader has been waiting—he wants to make sure I'm left with no time to disarm his explosives. This is his way of flushing me out.

The intervals grow shorter, almost in tandem with my rapid heart rate.

Once the beeping hits max speed, the Uuzik leader takes his leave, but not before glaring one last time in my direction.

Each step he takes down the path thunders out from under his bulky exterior. He fades into the mist. Finally, I'm left alone.

But it's far too late. He's sufficiently killed enough time so that I'll have no chance of disabling the bombs. Not that it matters in the end. I've already made the choice to sacrifice my ship in exchange for more time so that I can create a strategy.

That said, waiting in the misty forest and watching as each tiny bomb explodes one after another until my ship is fully up in flames stings. I duck for cover as shrapnel flies past me, each blast more ferocious than the last.

I'm lying on the ground, but I can hear pieces of metal whipping over my head and slicing through parts of the frail trees.

I give the situation a couple more minutes after hearing the last explosion, then check to make sure no Uuziks have returned before making my way up to the blazing fireball I used to consider a ship. Millions of tiny metal pieces are scattered along the ground like snowflakes, and bits of my roofing tiles are stuck in the trees, also on fire. The rest of the debris have likely ended up in the nearby bodies of water, never to be seen again.

I walk up to what remains of my ship, which is, in a word, nothing. I stare at it dejectedly. It's not just that my ship is in shambles — my hopes of a smooth escape have equally been obliterated.

"I knew this job would be the death of me," I curse under my breath in frustration. Honestly, I don't know what else to say. I'm stunned that I've managed to land myself in such a precarious position.

Not only am I stranded on some backwater planet in the

depths of the galaxy, but the Uuziks are roaming around as well, and they want my head for their trophy case now.

If that isn't enough, there's still one underlying issue that'll define my chances of survival more than anything else, and one that's getting more dire by the minute: my oxygen levels. If it runs out first, the Uuziks will have no need to worry about finding me…

I tap the side of my helmet to check the time.

18:00 hours left.

THERE ARE A LOT OF WORST-CASE SCENARIOS when you're a mercenary. Bounties on your head, the SFF probably tailing you at every turn, and plenty of unknown calamities lurking around each corner.

But all those minor worries pale in comparison to the situation I find myself in now. I'm left stranded on a planet not even registered in the SFF directory, with a bunch of intergalactic monsters who'd really enjoy removing my head from my shoulders. But the cherry on top is the doomsday clock looming above my head: my oxygen levels.

Even taking all that into account, there's still something that pisses me off more than anything else. If I make it out of this scenario alive—which, given my current predicament, seems unlikely at best—my spaceship insurance will skyrocket. Believe me, they don't take your ship being blown into millions of tiny pieces lightly.

After taking the appropriate time to grieve my situation and curse the Uuziks for the role they've played in it, I come to accept that I'll be stuck on this dirt ball of a planet a little longer.

Of course, I wouldn't be the mercenary I am if I were to just sit around and wait for death to claim me. I need to come up with a plan.

Since I've arrived on RG-87, I've yet to come across a single intelligent lifeform except for the Uuziks (though I'm loathe to actually call them intelligent).

That most likely means if there's other intelligent life on this planet, they're either in hiding or they're dead, but more than likely the latter considering the Uuziks are involved. So finding help is out of the question. The only exception I can think of is if someone else happens to be stranded here as well. But then again, that would just keep me from dying alone and wouldn't help much else.

While trying to decide my next steps, I remember something rather interesting the leader of the Uuzik said before blowing up my ship: "If it's a Fed, kill them immediately. Do not let them get anywhere near the facility."

So there must be some sort of Uuzik base on this planet then…and it has to be nearby.

I figure it's a safe assumption that the Uuziks picked this place because of how relaxed the Federation is when it comes to patrolling these outer planets.

More importantly though, if they had a facility built, that would require manual labour and resources, which would require transportation. Their base must be stacked with ships. Ships — which are my ticket out of this hell.

I start to follow the footsteps of the Uuziks while avoiding any rushed movements. Since the Uuziks took the original path I used when leaving the forest, I pull up my map and circle where I think they'll be. Then I mark my best route to avoid being seen and follow it to a T.

Also, my scanners will keep me aware of any nearby Uuziks who continue to search for me.

The fog still proves to be a nuisance—my view of the Uuziks keeps fading in and out—but I know at the same time it's also keeping me hidden. In a contest of instincts and stealth, I know I have the advantage compared to a race predicated on brute force and no subtlety. From what I can tell, there are six Uuziks within a mile radius of me, each one branching off and scouring every inch of the forest. This makes eluding them much easier than I expect. I stick to my route and play it cautious until I can begin to see the fog loosening up, which is the signal that I'm getting close to the edge of the forest. I check my map and see I'm on the Northwest side.

Finally, I hit the clearing, and my annoyed eyes take in a group of Uuziks about 50 meters away from me. They're standing in a circle talking amongst themselves, but I can't pick up what they're saying. Not that it matters; I'm far more interested in the machines parked in a nice line beside them. Hoverbikes.

They're shorter than the ones I used to ride growing up with the Federation, and a little bulkier as well, most likely so they can carry the cargo strapped on the machines' backs. It's box frame, and thin wires stretching from front to back make them appear quite flimsy, but at this point, I could care less. If it can float and has an engine, then it's checked off all my boxes.

The Uuziks break off and return to packing up their bikes, which gives me a couple more minutes to plan things out. From the look of them, I assume the bikes are easy enough to ride. And besides, if an Uuzik can figure it out, I have no doubt that I can.

First I need to get my hand on one of those bikes before they take off, but I also need to remain cognizant of the few Uuziks still searching the forest behind me.

In the final wave of bushes before miles of dirt, I crouch down and rest my hand on my pistol. I'm ready to strike at any moment.

But it seems too obvious. Even if I manage to kill them, the sound of my gun will alert others in the forest. I really need to get some sort of silencer for my pistol…

On the other hand, my photon knife needed to be close range. It's a four-on-one fight, and I have no interest in those odds.

Fraught with turmoil about what to do, my plan of action suddenly comes to light. And, even better, it requires no action on my end.

Screeches hail down from the desolate sky. I remember these all too well, and frankly I'd hoped never to hear them again. I turn my gaze to the clouds, peering through the weaving branches to catch a glimpse of this furry red and black body shooting downward like a rocket. It's only in my view for a second or two, but when I follow the persisting screeches to the Uuziks' little camp, I see mayhem breaking loose.

Let me tell you: Of the many different gods that are believed to be in control of our destinies, the god watching over mine is clearly a fan of toying with me. From coming up with all sorts of ways to throw my plans off course, now this same god smiles down upon me—as a dorneal. And an angry one, at that.

The same kind of enormous bird that nearly brought me to the edge of death comes crashing down in the middle of the Uuzik camp. The ground rattles, and I grab a branch to steady my balance.

One unfortunate Uuzik soul is the doomed landing pad for this dorneal, and is squished to a certain and painful death. I slink back into the bushes, putting my gun away. The other Uuziks begin an assault to avenge their fallen brother—or, more likely, to save their own skin, as is the Uuzik way—but they're about to learn a lesson that I already know well. An angry dorneal is not a creature to be messed with.

This one is even bigger than the one I fought, and it's out for blood. I wonder if this one is a fully grown dorneal, and the one I killed only a child. Perhaps this was the parent of that infant bird. I don't really like to consider that I might have killed a baby, but my options were slim at the time, and I really had no choice in the matter.

The Uuziks draw guns from their waists and start pummeling yellow beams of light toward the dorneal's crescent-moon-shaped symbol on its chest. But similar to my feeble attempt, these blasts do nothing more than provide a nice warm massage for the bird's fur.

Still, the threat gets the dorneal worked up. It starts fiercely stomping about while ripping up the ground with its long talons. It kicks its left leg out, and two of the Uuziks are impaled by its talons. I wince and look elsewhere, knowing how close that was to being me. Like a skewer, the dorneal shakes the Uuziks, throwing them off and leaving them dead in a pool of their own purple blood.

The winged beast starts to hover about a foot off the ground, flapping its wings furiously to create a windstorm that forces even me to hang on for dear life. The Uuziks have no chance—they're tossed dozens of feet through the air and land with a bone-shattering crack.

This is perfect, and I'm finally catching the break I need, but there's another calamity afoot: The bikes—my transportation out of there—are beginning to topple over. Their tied-up supplies meet a similar fate as the Uuziks, sailing high into the sky before tumbling down into a heap. Unfortunate, since I likely could've found some useful stuff in those boxes, but my priority remains fixed on the bikes not being obliterated.

*No! Leave the bikes alone, you bastard!* I think, as if I have any control over it.

The dorneal lands back on the ground and picks apart one of the dead Uuzik bodies nearby, until I see someone who I thought had left the forest long ago.

Out from the clearing stomps the Uuzik leader with two other of his men a step behind him. He storms toward the bird, accelerating to a rapid run. He shows no signs of fear, and for some reason this only serves to put more terror into me.

On the other hand, a part of me is intrigued to see how strong this Uuzik tyrant is against such a ferocious creature.

There's some logic behind this. If I'm to escape, it more than likely means I'll cross paths with such a brute, and it would do me well to gain any advantage I can. Not shockingly, he doesn't disappoint, which is bad news for me.

He grabs his gun, which looks a fair bit bigger than those of his lackies, and takes two clean shots, striking the dorneal in the face. Unlike the previous blasts, his shots squarely penetrate the beast, and streaks of green blood trickle down from the two fresh wounds under the dorneal's eyes. I wonder how he found a weapon with that much strength. Unlike my pinpoint shot to the enemy's eye, he just overpowered it with sheer strength, and it wouldn't be his last display of that same tenacity.

As the dorneal lands with a ground-shaking thud, it refuses defeat, taking a half-hearted swing at the Uuzik leader with its wing. A wasted effort.

The leader of such a violent race is not to be messed with, and one can tell this from his cocky strut as he moves in for the kill. In one last ditch effort to survive, the dorneal thrusts its talon forward, hoping to pierce its attacker's chest. But that would be the last of such hopes. The Uuzik catches the talon in his thick, muscular arms inches before it strikes true. He tightens his grip, muscles bulging as the dorneal lets out a painstaking cry for help. I remain in hiding. There's nothing I can do.

Crack.

The dorneal's cry reaches an almost unbearable octave before it finishes, collapsing in pain.

Like a tree branch breaking in half, the tyrant Uuzik snaps the dorneal's talon clean in half, leaving a bloody mess in its place. But he's far from done with inflicting torture. Like I said before, Uuziks only care about strength and power. They show no mercy when it comes to protecting their own species, and for certain when attacking other species they deem inferior.

He jumps up and lands on the dorneal's neck, his new-found weapon gripped tightly in his hand. He holds it high above the bird's head, picking the precise spot to jam his stake into.

For some reason, I want to help. I want to jump out and fight the tyrant in this moment, and I don't know why. I killed a dorneal as well, but that was because I was out of options. Had the bird flown away or been downed and still lived, I would have gladly left it alone. This just seems like torture. The Uuzik has won the battle, and he and his brood could go off back to whence they came and let the bird live. But, as established, this is not the Uuzik way.

Instead, the Uuzik proceeds to sink the dorneal's broken talon into its neck, watching it squirm in pain until it's finally delivered the sweet relief of death. For a second, I think that maybe the overkill tactic was an act of revenge for his fallen comrades, but the tyrant's hollowed expression says otherwise. He was doing it strictly because Uuziks don't leave things alive. He has no care in the world for his lost battalion.

After the ordeal ends, the remaining Uuziks and their leader pack up whatever supplies are left and mount their speed bikes, soaring off over the horizon.

Finally, I'm left safe and solitary. With the comfort of knowing this, I step out of the bushes, but not before taking one last look around to make sure the coast is clear. Everything checks out, and I hurry over to the Uuzik camp, or, more aptly, the wreckage site, and scour for any salvageable materials. Of course, nothing worth taking is left behind by the Uuziks, which I'd fully expected anyway.

They do, however, leave me one small parting gift, one I consider a mild retribution for them blowing up my ship.

To my left, lying next to the dorneal's corpse, is a hoverbike. Mind you, taking one look at the thing and still calling it a hoverbike might be a bit of a stretch. There are chips and dents all over the frame from being tossed around by the dorneal, and some of the base wires that stretch from the handlebars to the footholds have snapped off.

In my limited experience with hoverbikes, I can assess that the damage will likely make my ride less stable, but with any luck it should still run, which is more than enough for me.

I stand the bike upright and then give it a once over to make sure I detect no further damage. Nothing of note, but I do realize that this bike looks a fair bit different than anything I've ever ridden before. Not that I care, though; if I can get it up and running and it has even a fraction of fuel, that's more than enough for me to get started.

I sling my left leg over the seat before taking a some-what-paranoid glance behind me. I can't help it; I have to ensure no unwanted visitors are on my tail.

With nothing behind me, I take a look at the sky, this time to confirm no more dorneals are about to swoop down seeking revenge. Once I'm assured of my safety, I turn my attention to the square, holographic panel float-ing between me and the shaft of the bike's front jet. I glare at it, puzzled; I'm not understanding the language writ-ten on the screen. Also, the holographic display has two circles gradually floating back and forth like a screensav-er, but with words in the middle. At least I think they're words. One of them has to be "ignition," but I have no way of knowing.

For whatever reason, perhaps because it's a moving target or a holographic touchscreen, my visor struggles with any sort of translation of the text. It comes back with cryptic symbols, the same ones that have appeared the few other times I've seen error codes on my visor.

Left with little choice, I place my hand on the left-most circle and pray that nothing bad happens. A small push back like a burst of air hits the middle of my hand. I press further until I see the circle light up and a new menu open. One circle is green, the other red. This one is fairly obvious to me, even if I can't understand the Uuzik language. I press the green circle down, and this time I hear a spark from the ignition. My feet lift off the ground, and the bike starts to cough out billowy, thick smoke.

"Bingo. Now we're in business. Let's take this bad boy for a spin, shall we?" I muse aloud. When you work alone almost all the time, you tend to talk to yourself often. At least, I sure do.

Almost all hoverbikes handle the same way, which is a design factor that leans in my favour. Over the years, I've come across several different designs for vehicles. Some transport vehicles on more primitive planets use a gas and brake pedal for driving, while others can hook straight into your mind and react to your mental instructions instantly. Those can be tough to control, though.

Currently, the bike I sit on has no such apparatus. Instead, there are two handlebars with grips that can be held down. The one on the left is the gas, the one on the right is the brake. I place my hand on the left handle and give the gas a gentle squeeze. Unlike the Uuziks who blasted off at high speed and with a majestic roar of their engines, when I begin to move my machine lets out an ugly, sputtering cough as if it inhaled something the wrong way. It belches out another obnoxious sound and takes off at a turtle's pace.

Whatever the case may be, I have a working ride…more or less. As long as it remains functional, I can head to my next destination. But that brings up another question: Where is my next destination?

If there's an Uuzik base somewhere on this planet, then that's obviously where I need to go. But I have no clue where it could be, and RG-87, although small, isn't small enough for me to traverse the plains and just stumble upon it.

Although a dangerous decision, I settle on catching up with the Uuziks who took off moments before me. I know if I get to close, they'll turn around and put me out of this misery, but if I can get within range for my visor to track them, I stand a chance of following freely.

Of course, I need my bike to pick up the pace if I'm to stand any chance of chasing them down. I grip the handle and squeeze it all the way. My bike skips in the air for a moment, bellowing out a smoky sputter, but once it exhales whatever's clogging up the engine, my bike takes off.

I soar toward the horizon, unsure of what awaits me on the other side.


Much to my good fortune, my plan works better than anticipated. I'm still far enough away that I can't see the Uuziks, which means that they can't see me either. However, on the tip of my visor's scan range, I can still see red dots, which I know are the riders up ahead.

If I keep this up, I know I'll eventually stumble upon some sort of base. I have to.

A short time into my trip gliding along the dead soil of RG-87, I pull up my map, checking to see if any structures have been revealed. Much to my surprise, only one appears, and it doesn't look like a simple Uuzik base. First, it's far too big — almost like a tower-sized building. And second, it had loads of red dots scattered about on the inside, which are obviously all the Uuziks. And there are far more than I'd anticipated.

I'm still miles away, but after finishing my scan of the map, I veer to the east and begin traveling through a wide canyon. Large boulders are teetering on the edge of the canyon's lips, and if anything were to happen, they'd no doubt come crashing down on me.

I pick up speed, itching to get out of this potential death trap as soon as I can. Before long, I can see the Uuzik camp. But when you think of a camp site, or even a small base like a war bunker, you don't expect much, right?

This, as my map indicated earlier, is a steel kingdom of labour. The sun bounces off the metal walls that rise up to what I can only assume is about four or five floors. It has a cylinder shape that crawls up to the sky, and along the base are long, rectangular rooms, almost like a hanger. A hanger with ships, perhaps? There are also a number of branching-off rooms on the tower mirroring a tree with each room being a different set of branches. I can't even hazard a guess as to what those rooms contain.

What could the Uuziks possibly be doing on this planet

that requires such a massive yet intricate building? It's not like they're known for incredible technology or industrial prowess, so the fact that they could even build a tower so advanced on their own seems odd. But there it is, towering over me.

Two areas of the building are most intriguing to me. There's what appears to be a front door of sorts or some sort of garage entrance, and then the roof, which is an oval, glass dome, one that's plenty big enough to land half a dozen full-sized freight ships on. And one that I assume could also launch those half dozen freight ships as well. If my assumptions about the base floor of the towers holding their ships is wrong, then the roof would be my next best bet.

But getting to the top of the tower will be far harder than just getting through that large garage door.

I do a quick check on my oxygen supply. 17:12.

I still have plenty of time…for now.

The last thing that crosses my mind, and maybe the most interesting thing about a tower of this size and scale, is how it could be made under the noses of the Federation.

When it comes to the outer rims of the galaxy, I know the Federation is…well, let's just say fairly lax in their searches, but there's no way this place was built overnight. It must've taken some considerable time to stake out the land, understand its threats, and get materials onto the planet, not to mention the manual labour involved. Then again, perhaps at one point this planet wasn't as deserted as I'd thought.

I can't help but wonder if within that tower there are potential slaves working away on whatever nefarious plan the Uuziks have. There's a chance of that for sure, but it also doesn't seem like the Uuzik way. For all of the terrible and genocidal acts the Uuziks have committed over the years, they've never been one for taking in slaves from planets they've conquered. But, as you might have guessed, that wasn't just them playing nice—they didn't keep slaves because they'd just kill off the species, making room for more of their own kind.

All of it reminds me of home. After the Uuziks were through with my planet, Earth, anyone who traveled there would find it in a similar state to RG-87. Not as decrepit, maybe, but still just as barren and lifeless.

Though this is the Federation we're talking about here— they're not always the most competent bunch in the galaxy when it comes to picking up on subtleties. It's not out of the realm of possibilities that they just ignored this place.

Regardless, once I get close enough to the tower, I veer off to my right into a section of tall rocks—my hiding spot. The tower is surrounded by flat land, with only small sections of rocks large enough to hide a small village.

Since this whole mission has been a catastrophic mess, my paranoia is at an all-time high. I look behind myself again, making sure nobody is following me, then double-check the map and scan my field of vision to ensure safety. Once again, the coast is clear.

Chances are that if any Uuziks are floating around the area, they're in the steel palace rather than roaming the lands, but that would only make my task all the more difficult. I take a peek around the corner of my hiding spot, setting my eyes on the front door of the tower. A few Uuziks are entering, one of them being the tyrant himself. He's making strange gestures to the guard, and then a second one comes over and starts doing the same. He makes his way over to a panel on the far right and starts tapping a few buttons. It must be some sort of a security panel. After he finishes pushing buttons, the likely fifteen-foot wall of steel begins to split apart before concealing itself behind the interior of the tower.

The ground shakes as the doors scrape through their path, and I glance back up at the tips of the rock I'm crouched behind. Though they're not nearly as tall as the canyon's cliffs, if a boulder were to tumble down in my direction, it could most certainly kill me with ease.

Once I know I'm sufficiently out of sight, I whip my head back toward the fortress and its leader.

The door now fully open, the tyrant and his select group of minions disappear inside while the one remaining behind readies himself to seal the entrance shut once again.

Based on a rough calculation in my head, the steel doors take at least seven minutes to pull entirely apart. So the same amount of time for it to fully close again seems like a safe bet.

But if I'm to pull off my infiltration plan, I need to have impeccable timing. Too fast and I'll likely be caught by the Uuziks that just headed in. Who the hell knows what would take place if that were to happen? Probably a firefight, in which I'd be drastically outnumbered. But if I'm too slow…well, that's an obvious one to figure out. I'll be back to square one.

Once I see the last Uuzik—the one working the panel—head in, I hop on my bike and gear up. I spring into action and hit the gas, while at the same time praying that my beat-up hoverbike won't cough up enough noise to reveal my presence and ruin my chances.

Scans say that the left side of the building, which just so happens to be the side I'm closest to, has no foot soldiers patrolling the area, so I choose my route accordingly and speed up along the left side. Even while hovering along the ground at high speeds, I can feel and actually see the ground shaking below me. It slows down my bike too, so I use my thrusters to pack a little extra punch. Rounding the corner, I ditch the bike, sending it flying into the distance before making a mad dash to the doors that are already three-quarters closed.

*Christ, my calculations were a little off,* I sputter as I attempt to get there in time. *Come on, you can make it!* At best, only four maybe five minutes have passed.

But thankfully, I manage to slide through the doors as they slam shut behind me.

I have no time to celebrate my success, though—I need to find cover before someone spots me. I roll to my left and duck behind a small group of crates that are tall enough to hide my entire body.

That, however, will be the last thing I know for sure regarding the hanger's layout. I knew where the crates are located, because I could see a sliver of light beaming in that direction as the doors closed, but now that they're sealed shut, I find myself shrouded in darkness.

But a pitch-black room will still work to my advantage. With just a thought of it, a wave of green overtakes my visor, lighting up the room around me.

Obviously, my suit has night vision as part of its technology. I mean, that's as basic as it gets for a merc. We spend a lot of time hanging around in the dark, whether waiting for client intel or for a far nastier reason. But regardless, being able to see in the night is always top priority.

But one look around the room and I quickly realize my initial hopes have been dashed.

Much to my disappointment, the hanger I've entered has no illusions of being a docking bay. There are no ships anywhere in sight. In fact, based on the massive amount of crates that line the room, along with various machines to move them, I'd say I'm in their supply warehouse—whatever those "supplies" might be.

That said, I'm inside the fortress, and I can at least begin exploring and start working to find my escape plan. I still hold out hope that the rooftop will have a ship or two available.

Each step around the room is filled with a steady dose of caution. Although I do have a form of night vision, the strength it grants me isn't stellar. The path of light guiding my movements is no more than six feet from my face, which does little to provide me much time to react in dire situations.

Around the edges of the final line of crates, I start to hear the same low-grumbling chatter from back when I was hiding in the bushes. I sneak around and pop my head through a narrow crack in the crates. The tip edge of my range picks up two Uuziks standing in front of a rounded door. I press my back up against the crate and try to catch their conversation. It's faint, but I get a signal.

"The boss claims he saw Federation scum snooping around the forest," the one grumbles to the other. "His ship's toast, but they didn't find anybody on board. He thinks they'll be coming here next, if he hasn't already.

We need to run a sweep of every floor in the factory and dispose of any unwanted vermin."

The second Uuzik shakes his head in annoyance. "Of course we do. I don't get who put him in charge."

"You're more than welcome to bring that one up to the boss if you like."

The second Uuzik throws up his claws, "Fine, whatever. I'll sweep this floor. Chances are, if there is a Fed snooping around base, they wouldn't be in here anyways. Go check the labs on the second floor and see if you can find anything." He gruffly spouts off a few more annoyed words before stalking away.

I'm disappointed (but not shocked) that they know I'm around their base. It's not like I had much choice. And besides, all this really means in the end is that I lose my element of surprise, at least to an extent. They still don't have a scent on my exact location, so I definitely have a chance. But I need to remain cautious and avoid disaster. I'm in enemy territory, after all.

Although I have no way of confirming certain knowledge at this time, I recall hearing rumors on a couple different missions about Uuziks and their excellent night vision. It starts to make sense. Even with zero light around, they're maneuvering through the crowded crates with ease.

Then again, that would explain why nobody bothered to install a lamp or two in the darkest room you can imagine when building this mammoth tower.

Unfortunately, this also means any advantage I might've otherwise had with my night vision visor proves obsolete. If anything, I'm at a disadvantage, because the Uuziks sight range probably far exceeds my own.

For the time being, the best I can do is play hide and seek, which will be fine as long as no other Uuziks show up.

After the other guard walks through the door, I make my plan. First, I move to the other side of the crates, listening for the sounds of heavy footsteps. Thankfully, Uuziks don't walk like humans; there's no mistaking their thud-like footing. Seeing through the crates is nearly impossible, so I hazard a guess that the Uuzik guard is on the opposite side of my crate. He continues walking past me, not bothering to look back. He's still groaning to himself.

I move down the line of crates, distancing myself from the guard while also keeping one eye on him at all times. He's beginning to make his rounds through the room, and he's less than enthusiastic.

Since I dove into the hanger without much chance to survey my surroundings, I decide now would be a good time to get a lay of the land. After all, I don't want to get caught in a pinch and not know where I can run for cover.

The room itself is broken up into three sections. I'm in the area in the left, and on the right, I can see that there are crates stacked upon crates. In the middle of the room is a long, runway strip, wide enough for two small vehicles to go back and forth.

Why would they have this many crates kicking around here? Is this some sort of food supply for them? Or are they still working on building this place out?

This is one time that I wish I actually knew more about the Uuziks as a race. What do they eat? Do they eat? How do they survive? Considering the state of RG-87, it's not like they're growing their own crops or funneling water. At least not outside.

I guess in the end it doesn't make any difference regarding my escape, but part of me is curious how they can pull off such a plan.

The Uuzik guard marches back and forth up the center runway. He doesn't bother checking any of the crates—he just keeps walking, shaking his head in disgust.

Although his orders are to search for me, it seems obvious he doesn't care to be taking orders from his tyrant leader. I can't blame him on that front. I'm not big on following orders either.

He walks past me a second time, still unaware of my presence. I scurry like a mouse to the other end of the crates, beating him to the opening. I wait for the moment he passes me again, and then I make my move.

Like a stealthy thief in the night, I leap out from behind the crates and wrap my arms around his disgusting mouth and neck. He struggles wildly, doing all he can to stab me with his claw-like hands, but they aren't sharp enough to pierce my armour. Before he can come up with a plan of action, I sink my photon knife into the nape of his neck, feeling his strength slowly fade, just like the life in his body. Nothing but faint gasps and silent screams permeate the air.

As soon as he goes limp, I remove my knife, carefully placing his revolting body on the ground.

I won't say that killing an Uuzik, one of the vile creatures that ravaged and destroyed my home planet— gives me a feeling of satisfaction, but it doesn't come with the same sadness that I felt after the dorneal fight. As far as death is concerned, the Uuziks have it coming.

I shove the thought of the Uuzik killing to the back of my mind; a blood-lusting rage or hunt for revenge will do nothing more than get me killed. And besides, if I can find a way off this damn planet and warn the Federation of what's taking place right under their noses, that would be more than enough satisfaction for me.

I look down at my dark deed and the blood pooling on the floor, which I have no way of cleaning up. That's not a good sign, but I can't do much about it. The body on the ground, though — that can be disposed of. The last thing I need is to leave such an obvious literal red flag on the ground. As they say, nothing sets off alarms like the dead body of a comrade.

I heave the dead Uuzik over my shoulder and begin to assess my choices for a burial site. I realize that being in a room full of large crates will aid me in my quest. I crack open the lid of the nearest one and toss the body inside, ready to slam it shut like a coffin.

But then something inside catches my eye. I check to confirm that no other guards are coming by, and then I fully crack the top of the lid off.

Along with the dead corpse I stuffed in there, what I'm seeing shouldn't be a surprise, but in the drama of the moment, it certainly shocks me. Packed at the bottom of the box are crystals, crystals by the hundreds. But not just any ordinary crystals. Calax Crystals. The most highly reactive crystals in the galaxy, and I'd just casually tossed a body on top of them. I'm probably lucky I didn't blow up half the planet with that level of carelessness, but rather than worrying about what didn't happen, I have other questions that need answers. I crack open the crate beside me, and inside I see just as many Calax Crystals, all neatly lined up like a perfectly designed pyramid.

There must be enough of these things here to blow up a chunk of the universe. What the hell could the Uuziks be planning? Oh. Oh, no…even they wouldn't try that…

If there's one thing that always comes to mind when you think of Uuziks, it's their hatred toward the SFF.

Now listen: I hate the SFF, too. Anyone and everyone would tell you that. But compared to the Uuziks, I'm the SFF's best friend. And with this much firepower sitting in a dormant state, if the Uuziks can figure out how to properly utilize such explosive strength, they'd be able to blow the SFF away — not to mention the other ten planets in the solar system along with it. And all with just a brief snap of their claws.

For a split second, I think to myself, serves the SFF right for being so careless. But I refuse to be so petty. There are far too many innocent lives at stake for me to sit idly by and let them get the justice one could argue they deserve.

My desire to get off this planet has suddenly become much more urgent. I need to inform the Federation of this death-wish plan, while also pointing out their glaring oversite of monitoring this place.

Fear firmly planted in my mind, I close up both lids and decide to head on my way. There's nothing else notable I can see in the hanger, and certainly no options around to escape this desolate rock. Along with that, due to the sheer number of crates stashed away, I can't do much about what's already been harvested. All I can do is prevent them from putting such power into action. So I keep moving forward.

Through the next door, I find myself in the central room

of the tower. What's more, I have light again. I move to my right where there's a control panel booth for me to hide in. Because the Uuziks were kind enough to build a roof on their little kiosk—though for what, I have no idea—I'm covered from any aerial view, and I'm also able to duck down and sneak a look from the cut-out window in the front when I need to.

The base has a much more high-tech appearance than what the outside suggests, with green and red lines crawling up and down every wall like varicose veins. That must be their way of sending power to each room, but I really have no clue how it works.

As the outside suggests, the main tower is a long cylindrical shape, rising up with doors scattered about on each floor. Two branching paths go around the outside walls, but are cut short before you can walk the entire outer rim of the room. The only way to get across from one side to another is with the bridge that stretches across the middle. Each floor going all the way up has a similar look to it, but with the bridges angled slightly different.

However, when looking up from the bottom, the tower feels far more daunting.

Although I gauged how tall the building was before, what I failed to anticipate was that not only did the Uuziks build the tower upward, but also downward into the core of the planet as well. With a glance down, I estimate another two floors, though that is nothing more than a guess.

Bridges are the only way to get across to other floors, and if you're tossed over them, you'd be falling to what I figure is the core of the planet, not that I have any intentions of seeing what sort of mess is going on down there.

This is mostly because the chances of ships being located in some underground bunker seems slim to me, and I have no time for frivolous exploring. My destination continues to be the top floor, and I need to get there in a hurry.

Even more unsettling than the possibility of being tossed overboard to an infinite drop is the number of Uuziks marching back and forth on the upper floors like trained guards. These are not the only ones kicking around, though. More Uuziks are walking in and out of different doors carrying boxes of what must be Calax Crystals, or maybe other important supplies.

Because so many Uuziks are lurking on the floors above me, movement will be next to impossible. The only good sign is that none of them are on the first floor. I figure that the ones who are looking for me already checked this floor first and found nothing of note, which means they left it vacated. They also must have had a number of guards searching the planet's surface for me as well, since nobody can confirm if I'm inside or outside. Like I said, not the smartest spices in the galaxy, despite what they'd like to believe.

My opening now decided, all I need to do is make my move.

Counter-clockwise around the room are a few different doors, all with green lights pulsating around them. I can only hope that green means that they're unlocked. If it doesn't, I'll be caught with my pants down…but luckily, I'm right. I pick the closest door and slip on in before anyone can notice me.

I have my gun drawn and at the ready, but the game of roulette spins in my favour once again—somewhat. No Uuziks are to be found, which is an obvious point for me, but there are no ships or signs of them anywhere in here either. A point for the Uuziks.

Coming here isn't entirely without benefit, though. First off, I'm alone. And second, the long rectangular room has two rows of computers sitting on narrow desks, reminding me of an old, high school computer lab. Beside each computer is a small empty beaker and canister with broken shards of crystal floating in a strange blue liquid. At a glance they look ordinary enough, but when I pick up one of the jars to examine it, I realize what's inside. Without a doubt, they're running different tests on Calax Crystals. Due to the nature of the chaotic energy source, and despite the fact that they have a small village's worth of it, without learning to harness the power first they can't do much more than act as a bunch of martyrs.

Since I've already stumbled upon this room and it provides some interest, I want to make sure I have time to examine every last detail. I clean off one of the long desks, making sure not to accidently react the crystal supplement, and then I shove the desk in front of the door I've just entered.

If the door was to open, it would do little to protect me from blaster bullets, but it would buy me some time to gain my bearings before the Uuziks start to flood in. Hopefully I can examine this room and get out before being noticed. That'll spare me a lot of headaches.

With the room secured, I walk behind the second untouched row of desks and take a seat in front of the nearest computer. If I can find a way to hack into their system, perhaps I can gain some map data or, better yet, security cameras which will tell me if my hunch about the roof is accurate. But in my haste to gather information, I overlook one minor detail.

I hear a strange chime to my right, like a door being unlocked. I look toward the sound's direction—the opposite of where I've placed my obstructive desk—and see a second door.

The colour changes from red to green. I put aside the desire to kill myself for committing such a careless act and dip under the desk. Like the last Uuzik I came across, this one is another grumpy, under-appreciated minion with a chip on his shoulder. I'm beginning to see a trend in how Uuziks feel about their own kind and their leaders. But that plays right into my hand.

Either through another lucky break or just careless disinterest on the part of the incoming apparent scientist, he pays no mind to the blockade I've created and instead sits at the computer terminal on the far end from me.

Instead of going in for the kill right away, I decide to wait and let him do the tough work for me. A few keystrokes later and a ton of grumbling (which my visor picks up as gibberish), he logs in and ends up, unbeknownst to him, granting me access to valuable information. Hopefully.

Like a ninja, I pop out from the shadows of the desk and stab the Uuzik in the back of his prehistoric-shaped head. A quick, clean, and—most importantly—silent kill that won't draw suspicion.

But this time I have no place to hide my deed. No crates are around and there are no other suitable places to dump a body. I kick the limp corpse out of the chair, and it stares up at me from its carved-out eye sockets. I don't plan on being in this room for long, so hopefully it doesn't matter that he's splayed out in plain sight.

I take my seat once again and began looking through the different Uuzik files on their system. Navigating an unfamiliar source of technology is tricky enough, but when I can't understand the language it's next to impossible. I keep clicking on different icons looking for any files to pop up that might be useful, but for the most part they're just images of Calax Crystals with some Uuzik-language writing underneath them.

My luck runs short on my quest for map data, but what I do find sets off some other red flags about this Uuzik's plans, leaving me more than a little perplexed.

What the Uuzik scientist was loading up before I stole his life was a folder labeled "Project BB." No snooping was required for these notes—the file popped up on its own, begging me to read it. Along with the notes, I see a number of dated logos providing more insight.

---------------------------------- LOG DAY 187, PROJECT BB

**Although still in its infant state, the project has been coming along at a rapid pace. Our first estimate of 352 days for a full-term completion appears to be an overestimation by a wide margin. While still growing through the infant stage, the Calax Crystals continue to provide a source of nutrients for the weapon. Once we move on to the next stage, we expect the process to pick up speed further. However, this means we will need to**

**continue harvesting Calax Crystals by the hundreds if we are to keep pace.**

---

I scratch my head. Project BB? And it's using Calax Crystals as a source of energy? Does that mean the Uuziks have been designing some sort of super weapon? And with the amount of crystals they've already harvested? If this is a recent log, then I can't even fathom how dangerous this machine could be. But the biggest question here is…how far along have they come in creating it?

I want to continue my discovery of this weapon they've dubbed BB, but some spine-chilling low grumbles near the other door snap me out of my readings.

I need to find a hiding spot, and quick. My eyes rapidly scan the room, rejecting all options, until I see a metal grate cut into the bottom corner of the wall.

The ventilation system. I run over and grab the bars, popping them off with ease and then making my way in. The vents are spacious enough for me to crawl on my hands and knees, but turning around will be next to impossible unless they open up somewhere else.

To make sure I'm not spotted, I'm forced to go in backwards; that way, I can lift the grate back into place. Once I do that, nobody will be the wiser.

After I pull off my plan, I hear the unblocked door chime open and see two Uuziks come through. I start crawling through the vents, contorting my body until I can situate myself. And I can't make a single noise while I'm doing it. Trust me — with a metal suit clanging up against metal vents, noise is bound to happen.

But I do what I can, and once I'm spun around, I start crawling along the metal floors as if I'm back in Space Federation training.

I move up along an arching slant, seeing only green from my visor before finding myself up above the ceiling. As I crawl along the metal, I try to remain as silent as a mouse.

Soon I come across a ceiling vent. A chance to pick up some more information presents itself, so I choose to take it.

Below are two Uuziks at the computer I was at previously. They're kneeling over, examining something on the ground. A body. A body I may or may not have shoved my photon knife into and tossed to the side in haste. Normally, I'd never be so careless on an infiltration mission, but all things being fair, it's not like there were a lot of places to hide the body.

But now the Uuziks are on high alert, which will cause all sorts of headaches for me.

The two are having a conversation below that I listen in on:

"Report back to the boss. Tell him the Federation soldier has breached the building and is killing our men."

The second Uuzik, who appears to be younger as he's a few inches shorter than the average Uuzik, looks at the dead body and then back to his comrade, or even perhaps his superior in the Uuzik hierarchy of power. His eyes widen, and for the first time I actually see what I think might be fear in an Uuzik's swollen, beady eyes. Is he scared that on his way to the boss he might cross the blood thirsty path of a Federation soldier, or is he more scared of the tyrant? I was about to get my answer.

"Why do I have to report back to the boss? If I tell him, we let the Federation solider into the building he'll have my head!"

"You can either tell the boss on my orders, or you can end up like this guy." He lifts his claw up and points it at the young one's neck, letting the tip graze his scaly skin.

Such a threat will be enough for the young Uuzik to take his leave from the room back out to the main bridges.

As they disperse, the first one looks up to the vents I'm hiding in. I nearly leap back in shock, and if I had any room in there, I would.

Did he see or possibly hear me opening the grate and assumed I went into the vents? I have a lot of speculative questions, but I take a deep breath, steady myself, and decide if they're about to go on high alert, I need to start making my way up the floors in a hurry.

Since they found the body on the first floor, with any luck, maybe they'll flood the area and give me a chance to move around more freely. Blind hope, I guess.

As soon as the other Uuzik leaves the room, I start to crawl toward my next destination. Not that I have any clue where that'll be, but hopefully it's less cramped.

The Dynex suit has three main ways of getting information and processing it. The first is as simple as the galactic web. I can run a mental search and draw any information from a wide array of sources. This is always great for discovering random knowledge. The second is through data chips that I can upload to my suit. These can include encrypted data and other highly classified information. Most of the time, anything of that nature would be provided to me before a mission's start, such as a map of the area, but with no foresight of my current predicament, there's no chance of that happening.

If I can get my hands on a map data disc, it would be

my best bet of getting a full map of this place. But this seems unlikely.

The third way of gathering data is by simply exploring and logging information myself, the same way I did to start building map data on RG-87's surface. But, again, that does little to help my current situation.

Instead, I'm forced to go off memory while I travel through the vents. There are far more turns and four-way intersections than I anticipate, but if my mind's eye had drawn the map of the first-floor layout, then I'd be parallel with the converging bridge that connects this room with the one on the other side. I keep crawling forward until I can see another grate hanging from the ceiling of the room. I run a quick scan to make sure the area is safe before I bail out of my cramped confinements.

There are no signs of Uuziks in this room, but that doesn't mean I'm alone. A few different oddly shaped life-forms pop up on my scan, causing me to pause. They're far smaller than an Uuzik.

Dangerous or not, I drop down looking left and then right to ensure that the room is clear. It is.

In the Uuzik facility, there are far more rooms than just a bunch for storage and computers, I quickly learn. The room I've dropped into is far from what I'd expected. Everywhere I look, glass containers and different exhibits are set up like a zoo.

One display is a giant tank of water, filled with different types of fish. Most look rather strange, but they're tiny and therefore most likely harmless. Other areas contain a small beach like sand trap, and a few different grasslands extended further into the room. I'm sure this is meant to be some sort of wildlife breeding ground, but I can't get the thought of a sad-looking petting zoo out of my mind, one with an eerie vibe to it. One in which every step you take, you know you're being watched by all the creatures.

It could be an interesting room to explore if I had the time, but with the clock continually counting down to my potential death, detours through a poorly built animal sanctuary are a bad idea. I need to start moving, so that's what I do.

There are two points of interest that I continue to scout around for, but I figure that both of them won't be in this room. Map data, as always, and any more information on this Project BB.

As expected, once I walk around the bend of the room and pass all the different exhibits, nothing relating to those two things presents itself.

The other end of the room has a similar oval door to it, but with a red glow around the outside. In other words, it's locked.

A small, circular window is carved through the steel door, which gives me a glimpse into what's being stored on the other side. But to my surprise, it's not another room or extension of exhibits—quite the opposite, actually. It's a staircase climbing upward to the next floor. With this being the case, my next step is to figure out how to unlock the door.

Before I make my way back, the innocent whimper of a small creature catches my attention. In spite of my brain thinking *Don't waste your time on this,* I figure that exploring won't be a complete loss; after all, if the Uuziks went to such trouble to capture these creatures, I should at least see what they're using them for.

The cry comes from my left, in a section of the zoo's

grasslands. A tall tree stretches out from a deep pit, and I lean over the railing, looking down and trying to spot the source of the sound.

On the fresh grassy floor, something I've not yet experienced on RG-87, there are piles of leaves and broken branches. The base of the tree also has an obscure, carved-out hole with claw marks and bark shavings along the ground trailing to the inside. The opening in the tree looks far from natural due to these claw marks; it's clearly been ripped apart with incredible determination.

I hear the whimper again, and this time I spot a pair of yellow eyes form within the darkness of its nestled home. The tiny creature sticks its head out while innocently grabbing at its floppy green and black oval ears. It looks around, once to the left then once to the right, as if judging if it's safe to leave its home. After it deems the coast clear, the wee being steps out of the hole in the tree before staring up at me. Those big yellow eyes lock with mine, and I can feel my heart melting from the cuteness that I'm witnessing.

------------------------------------- Treklet: Mammal, Male

**A small woodland creature known for having a ferocious appetite. Its furry exterior can change colour based on its surroundings in order to hide itself from predators. Treklets are often plant-eating animals, but when in limited circumstances or overcome with hunger can become carnivores.**

**Threat Level: 1.5 stars** ----------------------------------------------

I read the words as they scroll up my visor, but the details don't add up, particularly because the pictures displayed alongside the description differ from this creature that's now looking up at me. From what I can tell, a regular treklet looks more like a snow-white bunny, with big floppy white ears and a small round tail of similar colour. But the one standing below me has colours that make it look like military camo with its green and black spotted fur.

Now, because their fur can change colour due to various circumstances, I can let that part slide. But what I refuse to ignore is the long, winding tail that whips back and forth, or the unusually short but floppy ears this treklet sports. Also, as it grins, its mouth opens just wide enough for me to realize it has fangs. And not tiny little canine fangs—these things could rip through human flesh at a moment's notice. Is this a subset species of treklet? Not likely, I'd imagine.

A better guess would be that this poor creature has undergone various experiments or mutations at the hands of the Uuziks. Whether by a steady dose of Calax crystals or by some other means, this creature has endured some form of metamorphosis.

There's one other thing I fail to recognize at first, but once I do, I know something is up. Small parts of old treklet bodies are scattered about, some half buried in holes, others laying in the grass, but all of them mangled beyond the point of recognition. It looks like there are about seven or eight slaughtered treklets strewn about. I'd consider it a bit of treklet genocide, in all honesty.

But that leaves a few other lingering questions about the little fluffball below. Is the treklet starring back at me the cause of this graveyard, or had it been the Uuziks? Based on the damage to each of the creature's bodies — at least the ones still somewhat intact — the Uuziks must be to blame. Some of them had deep, scathing, scratch marks on them, while others had their chest cavities ripped open. The sight disgusts me a fair bit, and that's even considering everything a mercenary is accustomed to normally seeing.

I lock eyes with the seemingly cute and innocent treklet once again, but this time its pupils begin to thin until they're small slits. It lets out a ferocious hiss before lunging directly for my face. I hop back and reach for my gun before hearing a thud. The suddenly demonic treklet seems to have crashed into some kind of an invisible barrier before dropping down unceremoniously.

"At least the Uuziks are smart enough to contain the monster they made." I return my gun to my belt and shake my head.

There isn't much left to do for this poor little demon, so I figure now would be a good time to continue my exploration for a facility key.

As I make my way back, I can't help but wonder about the treklet and this mysterious Project BB. Are the two linked somehow? Is that treklet the "infant stage" they were referring to? It can't be, not at that size. Even with the little thing appearing so vicious, there's no way it can pose any sort of a threat, at least not to a planet worth threatening. And if it can't handle that job, then it would never come close to bringing any sort of harm, let alone taking down the Federation.

A further investigation is required, but with the clock ticking on my life expectancy, I need to keep moving.

Walking past a body of water that's enclosed like a fish tank, something catches my eye. It zooms past me, cutting through the water at high speed. Even though there's a barrier of protection, I can't help but remain on edge. The tank is huge, spanning at least ten meters, and is twice my height. Unlike the outside planet's mossy green and very likely toxic water, this water filling the tank is crystal blue, looking like it came straight out of a photograph.

One fish dwarfs all its brethren in the tank, swimming rapidly in and out of the coral reefs. I wonder if it's also undergone a transformation similar to the treklet. Perhaps the Uuziks are seeing how different creatures react to Calax Crystal energy. I've never heard of the crystals being used in animal experiments, only as a source of power, but at this point and with what little puzzle pieces I have at my disposal, there's only so much I can solve.

Once I reach the door on the other side of the terrarium, I realize quickly that it has the same set-up as the door to the stairwell; it's locked with a taunting red glow. That's when I remember I didn't come through a door, but through the ventilation system.

"Damn, they must've locked all the doors to make sure I can't escape. This could be a problem."

With no other solutions apparent and in dire need of an escape, I decide to hide for the moment and see if a poor soul or two comes looking for me. If I get lucky, perhaps I can either kill the unfortunate bastard or potentially sneak through the door unnoticed. And if that plan backfires, I guess I can always return to the vents, except that would keep me stuck on the first floor. I chalk this option up to a last resort.

I make my way back to the forested area of the terrarium

to stalk the stairwell door, but this time when I pass the treklet exhibit and give my new friend a casual glance, I notice an uncomfortable observation—one that could prove fatal if accurate.

I peer into the dome, checking every inch of the land, but there's no treklet to be seen. A bunch of treklet corpses, but nothing else. Is the treklet hiding in the tree? It couldn't have got out, could it?

A shiver crawls up my spine and then I spin around. Up, down, left, right—I look everywhere around me and then back into the dome to see if I've just missed the little bastard, but nope—it's just up and vanished.

I check to make sure the invisible barrier remains intact; when my metal fist clanks off the wall of light, I can confirm that it is.

This leaves me with three separate scenarios playing in my head.

The first, and good Lord, I pray that this is the case: I'm simply blind or my visor just isn't picking up anything in the dome. Maybe the little critter is just playing a game of hide and seek and bested me. That's one game I'd be okay with losing.

The second option seems possible in theory, but one I harbour serious doubts about: Somehow the malicious creature has escaped on its own. Whether by some means of digging out through the bottom or a lapse in the barrier I can't be sure, but either way, such an outcome would be dangerous.

The third scenario, and the one that seems most likely: Someone from another room shut off the barrier and let the wee monster free in hopes of possibly sniffing me out from my own hiding.

But if that's the Uuziks' plan, I'd say it failed. Wherever that treklet scurried off to, its level of interest in me is now seeming pretty low. With any luck, it'll go seeking revenge on the ones who turned it into such an adorable monster. I don't know if treklets are capable of such brain power, but it would certainly make my life easier.

Whatever the case, I've wasted enough time standing around. But my plans have changed now. Based on my hunch, the Uuziks let their experimental creature loose because they know I'm here, which means that waiting and hiding might be a really bad idea. No chance that they'd send only one or two people after me; odds are it would be the entire Uuzik fleet knocking on my door. If that happens, I'm screwed.

Cutting my losses, I start making my way back to the vents trying to visualize a map in my mind. I need to start planning where I'm going next.

But when I get halfway through the long room, I hear a strange munching noise.

It has a hard crunchy sound to it, like something biting into bark. I draw my gun and slow my pace, latching onto the sound and pursuing it. I take a look around as the munching grows louder. It sounds like it's coming from above, and it also carries a strange echo.

That's when I come across an unusual sight. There in the middle of the hall are two Uuziks. Except they're dead. And not only dead, but mutilated to the point of being almost unrecognizable. The one on my left had his face gouged, its blood pooling on the ground, while the other is missing most of his limbs.

Along with the pool of blood, streaks of it are absolutely painting the floor. This goes up for a few boxes until it disappears into an open vent. My vent.

I know I closed that thing. I must have. Christ, this might be trouble...

How one little treklet, mutated or not, has the power to kill two Uuzik guards baffles me, but going back into the vents is now a risk I can't afford. If I were to meet that treklet in a confined space with my movement hampered...well, I can't see it ending much better than this mess.

But, actually, the demon treklet has done me one massive favor. My original plan of ambushing some Uuziks turns out to be a success thanks to him. Here I am, standing over two dead Uuziks, and I didn't even have to get my hands dirty.

I kneel down and start searching what remains of the Uuziks' bodies. Thankfully, the treklet left one small item intact, and it's exactly what I need. I pluck a black rectangular key card off of one of the Uuziks' bodies and stand up.

Before I rush back to the stairwell with key in hand, I look back at the now-open vent. I can't help but get a bad feeling about the treklet...the damage it's capable of could be a problem, and these dead Uuziks are proof of that. If I were to cross paths with it again, I might have my hands full. Of course, that's if the Uuziks don't dispose of the creature first.

On the other hand, perhaps it could do me another favour and thin out the Uuzik ranks for me. That would at least make the little devil's escape worth my trouble. Clearly it doesn't care for its masters.

I make my way back to the door leading to the stairwell, but as I do, I continue hearing bumps from the ceiling above. The treklet is like a wild mouse scurrying around, and who knows where it'll end up.

One quick swipe of the key card into the left side of the door, and I watch with a renewed sense of hope as the light changes to green.

The stairwell zigs and zags up three flights to the second floor. I use the key card again to open the next room, but when I open the door, I find myself back in the room with the bridges. Just one floor up.

That's the good news. The bad news is that I'm in plain sight of anyone above me or across from me. Before I can make a move, I hear stomping footsteps that make the bridge feel like it'll collapse.

Rumblings that heavy couldn't possibly be created by a treklet running around—I'm wildly certain of that.

But I have a pretty good guess about the monster that could.

I need to act or else I'm a sitting duck, so I open the door to my immediate left with no regard for what could be on the other side. Each terrifying step, louder and louder, signals that the Uuzik tyrant is closing in on my position. It's only a matter of time until he gets a beat on my location. No doubt he's been informed of my intrusion on his terrarium and has decided to investigate himself.

I hurry through the door, taking less than a second to see if anyone else is around. I'd rather deal with the consequences of rushing into a room full of Uuziks than face that mutant.

The door slides closed behind me and I scan the room.

Thanks to chance or fate or whatever you want to call it, I see no one.

This room has the same dull metal interior as most rooms in the tower, but unlike the other one which was filled with computers and chairs like a workstation, this one's adorned with a series of long rectangular screens along the wall. For a second, it seems that I've entered some kind of Uuzik security system, and in a sense, I have, but the monitors aren't showing a variety of rooms like you'd expect. Instead, they display different angles on all of the exhibits in the terrarium room.

Each monitor shows a different section of the terrain, with animals big and small running about. There turns out to be even more than I noticed before. I wonder if there are multiple terrariums around this place and if this is the central place to watch them all. But I don't have time to be making random guesses.

Because before I can do anything, I need to block off the door. At least then I can buy myself some time.

Glancing around, I grab whatever heavy chairs I can find and jam them in front of the door, taking caution not to make any noise.

Just as I finish, the thunderous steps of the tyrant comes to a stop. I hide, my back pressed against the same wall as the door. I have a bit over 16 hours of oxygen left, but for a few moments I manage to extend that timeframe because I'm holding my breath for nearly a minute. The entire time, my hand remains on my gun, and knife is at the ready for my potential sneak attack.

I think I hear grumbling from outside, but I realize that my brain could absolutely be playing tricks on me.

I remain silent but constantly on edge. Eventually, though, the footsteps begin again. Fortune seems to smile down on me, however, because they're getting quieter as if they're departing.

A few more seconds pass and then the sounds of stomps fade entirely. I manage to evade capture once again.

I take this as my opportunity to check out the room further. Perhaps it can provide me with the information I'm looking for.

I sit at the controls, adorned with a bunch of basic buttons that are rather easy for me to navigate. They're mapped with common symbols for playing and rewinding video, so I take advantage of the resource and tap on the far-left button, causing the cameras to start rewinding.

I pause it at the exact point the ceiling grate swings down and I hop out of the vent shaft. This makes it abundantly clear that if any Uuziks were in this room in the last half hour, I'd no doubt have been spotted and guards alerted. Either nobody was monitoring this area or I'm walking straight into a trap. A trap I can't ignore.

Disregarding these concerns, I start to fast forward until the two guards make their inevitable and unfortunate entrance to the terrarium. They're heading toward me and the treklet sanctuary.

This must have been where I was attempting to find a hiding spot, because if I'd been any closer at the time, I would have heard some sort of commotion.

I can't make out how the treklet escaped, but I can only guess the barrier was deactivated. From watching the tape, the treklet climbs up the side of the wall but, unlike when it lunged at me, the little devil simply walks out freely. Then, strangely enough, the camera goes black for a few seconds, and when it goes back online the treklet is gnawing on the corpses of my Uuzik friends.

I have to admit that as much as I despise the Uuziks, watching the disgusting sight of their own creation sinking its long unnatural fangs clean through Uuzik armor makes me a little ill.

I fast forward until all that remains is the mangled mess that I'd stumble upon a few seconds later.

Then, just as suspected, the creature crawls up some boxes and leaps onto the vent grate, bringing it down, after which it crawls up and makes its daring escape.

Now, whether that will work to my advantage is yet to be determined. If it was indeed the dreaded Project BB or has something to do with it, it might be best to let the creature free. Anything that slows down the build of a super weapon has to be considered a win, right?

Of course, the other way to think about things is that I potentially just let a rabid, lethal weapon free, and the ramifications of that could be catastrophic. But at this point, I'm willing to take my chances.

I check the door again and see that nothing has changed — which seems obvious since I would have heard it — but by now, my paranoia is at an all-time high.

Regardless, I decide to push my luck further and see if I can dig deeper into their computers.

Beside the controls are a more basic touch pad and holo keyboard. I might not be able to read any of the keys, but there's one thing I notice in the top right corner of each screen: a small red X. I don't need a translation to know what this means, so immediately I run my finger across the touch pad until a cursor appears. Half a dozen clicks later, I make it back to the main screen. Just as before, I come to a plain blue screen with a bunch of folder icons scattered about. It's stunning to me that the Uuziks could build this entire fortress, but not one of them has any sense of file organization.

Ignoring these personal gripes, I click the folder that says "Project BB" on it. Subtle. I guess they weren't expecting anyone to stumble upon their computer lab, and therefore found no need to give the folder a cryptic name. When I open the folder, there are well over 300 files, each labeled in their native tongue. Since I can't decipher the names, I take my chances and click one at random.

-------------------------------------------------- **Project BB, DAY 227**

**The lifeform continues to grow at a steady pace. In the last few weeks, it has become even more destructive than we anticipated. An unexpected but intriguing discovery nonetheless. We have moved the lifeform to another location in order to keep it from wiping out our entire forces. It should only be a few more days until the Calax Crystal serum takes effect. Once that happens, the lifeform will begin to take on its next metamorphosis. This will be the true test. If the lifeform is able to sustain its new state, we'll begin development on the next stages.**

--------------------------------------------------------------------

So Project BB is undoubtedly a weapon, but still I don't have a description on what it looks like. What I do know is that as it grows, it's also becoming a threat to the Uuz-iks…the ones who are creating it.

The more I think on it, the more that devil treklet seemed like the ideal candidate for this Project BB. And now it's on the loose. Perfect.

Another thing that pops into my mind—and honestly, I can't believe I forgot about it—is that there's still a dozen ultra-powerful crystals sitting right under my armpit—the same things that the Uuziks are using to create such a vicious monster.

I know these crystals are powerful—anyone in the universe with half a brain knows that. But I'm starting to wonder if it's possible that the information we currently know about this stuff doesn't even scrape the depths of its powers. Think of it: to be able to transform such an innocent harmless creature into a killing machine…

Or, and as much as I hate to admit it, maybe the Federation does know the extent of the crystals' powers and actually predicted the danger. It would be a first for the SFF if you ask me, but would also make more sense about why they were outlawed on almost every planet in the galaxy—even for themselves.

To make matters worse, with the desperate need to escape before the Uuziks find me—along with the need to preserve oxygen—I'm starting to question just how good of an idea bringing these little crystals back to the Bacardi is. All I have to do is take into account my last few hours to see nothing good can possibly come out of this intense power source. That being said, going through this much of a hassle to not even get paid…

Putting my moral conundrum aside, my biggest priority remains the same: Avoid the Uuziks and get to the top of this damn tower.

After I do some more digging through their computers, I'm finally rewarded with data I've long hoped for. One of the folders contained blueprints of the entire facility, and even if it doesn't match the same 3D-model specs my map can produce, it's more than enough information for me to use. I find my bearings and start to navigate where I need to go and how to get there.

A single floor above me, there's an outline of a large circle. It resembles a landing pad, and it's connected to the rooftops. This gives me even more hope.

One floor up. That's all I need, and I'll no doubt find a spaceship, and with that, my escape.

For good measure, I pop out a small rectangular chip from the side of my helmet. I check for a slot to place it, which happens to be in the top-left corner of the holo keyboard. Once I plug it in, a small series of windows appears onscreen, and then a few loading bars. Thankfully, the map data takes no time to upload, and now I'm able to convert it into the full 3D-scale I'm accustomed to. For a moment I feel like I can smile, but that smile soon disappears.

As soon as the upload finishes and I rip the chip from the keyboard, the lights in the room flicker. My eyes shoot up to the ceiling and then instinctively back to the doorway before the lights change to crimson red. This is followed by a blaring alarm ringing throughout the building. It sounds like a fire alarm coming from every angle, and it's nearly deafening.

For a split second, I wonder if I accidently set off an alarm when I plugged my headset chip into the computer. I don't think the Uuziks would've allowed the data to be absorbed before setting the alarm, though.

More likely, the Uuzik tyrant has simply grown tired of hunting me himself and has put the place on high alert. Not that it matters one way or another. I know where I need to go.

I pull up my new 3D map and furiously examine the layout through flashing red lights.

If I were in a different situation, my suit would be able to muffle out the ringing of the alarm with relative ease, but because taking away my ability to hear would make monitoring for the Uuziks that much tougher, I don't activate it. Luckily, I don't need to hear myself think in order to use my map. I find my chosen path, which involves going along the bridge to the third floor, the floor that links to my destination.

Plan in place, I start to remove my barricade from the door.

I must admit, it seems strange that not one Uuzik has tried to enter thus far. It makes me wonder, but once I peek outside, I realize why I remain unbothered — and, more importantly, how.

Not only is the bridge that stretches across to my destination filled with piles of dead Uuzik bodies, but even the floor below has a few hanging off the edge like rag dolls. Also, some Uuziks are splattered up against the walls, but all of them look like they were sliced and diced just for fun. Basically, I've walked in on a modern day Uuzik genocide.

What could have done this much damage in such a short

time? No, it couldn't be that treklet. There's no way. There has to be at least thirty to fifty bodies around here.

A great opportunity descends upon me, and with the persistent ringing alarm, I can move without being heard. As long as I don't come across the tyrant, I'm freer than ever before.

I continue along the bridge slower than what would likely be advised. At any second, Uuziks could rain fire down from above, but for some reason I know that won't be happening. Call it a hunch, but I don't think the Uuziks care much about me for the moment. I also start to consider that the alarm might have nothing to do with me. Even the Uuziks know I could never cause this much damage or take this many lives. Although, who would have thought that one little woodland monster could, either.

For the first time since arriving on RG-87, I'm not considered the biggest threat to the Uuziks' plans.

The last obstacle remaining in my way is the door on the other side of the bridge. I try my key card, but it comes back with a red light. Denied.

I growl, definitely not in the mood to go searching again. Through an act of desperation, I draw my photon knife and stab and slice into the door, treating it like a turkey dinner until it's loose enough to kick down.

I see no reason to be stealth now that all hell is breaking loose. After all, this is a one-way exit for me, one through which I'll either die or finally escape this planet. It's hard to imagine any other outcome.

Just like the treklet before me, I leave a destructive path getting through the door and toward the staircase.

Up the stairs and around the bend, I finally see a glimmer of hope—the rounded room on the third floor. It looks like my guess from earlier turned out to be spot on.

The large oval room is a massive loading dock. Even better, there are more than half a dozen ships of different shapes and sizes, all parked in a nice row. A few solo pods, a couple two seaters, and even a strange looking transport ship, the likes of which I've only seen from big factory shipments and are mostly used for transporting materials from planet to planet.

But the solo ships are more than enough for me to escape on. Assuming I can operate them, at least. I just have to take my chances.

The sun faintly shines through the glass roof, blinding me as I look up. I lift my hands to shield myself from the rays, but as I do I feel my chest jolt backwards and a burning sensation on my left breastplate. Smoke rises and I spot a small singe mark on my suit. It absorbs the blast well, but I certainly don't want to be taking too many more shots like that.

I dive for cover behind the cargo ship as pistol blasts shower down around me like rain. The number of shots fired make it impossible for me to gauge how many Uuziks are storming in, but I'm guessing north of ten. They must have come in from the other side of the room to cut me off.

With my pistol in hand, I try to lean around the edge and pick off a few, but the Uuziks are closing in on me fast. All this while I'm a foot or two away from the cockpit of a massive carrier ship that calls out to me with the promise of freedom.

But if I try to hop in now and escape, I'd be nothing

more than a sitting duck as the ship takes the time it needs to start up.

For the time being, I return fire, my aim far outmatching the Uuziks. But where I have skill, they have numbers, numbers I can't compete with. And as if that isn't enough to contend with, my aim is thrown way of course as the ground suddenly shakes violently. Of the long list of problems in front of me, the biggest one has now appeared.

The reason the ground continues to shake, and the reason I can no longer aim straight, is the growing pain in my ass known only to me as the tyrant Uuzik.

He pounds the metal floor with each step, leaving imprints as he walks. I'm already in well over my head with my life on the line, but this is too much.

Deep in the back of my mind, the lingering thoughts of revenge remain. I can't forget the destruction of my planet, the death of my family, the people I never even got to know, and the many tragedies I can't ignore.

And now comes a prime opportunity to strike down the monster who caused it all.

I could make one final stand and get my revenge, but I know better. Now is not the time for my ego to get involved.

The firing comes to a stop, and for a moment I can breathe. Just for a moment.

The footsteps also cease, which prompts chills running down my spine. Something is about to happen, something that I'm definitely not expecting.

"Show yourself, dog," the metallic, brutish voice of the tyrant yells out with a deep roar. I'm shocked, not by the nature of his voice, but because the words are in plain English. Plain, angry English. I do a double take toward the corner of my visor and realize that my suit isn't running any sort of translation. The tyrant lord can speak English.

I guess I shouldn't be all that surprised. Although there are numerous different languages and dialects throughout the galaxy, most people on Dubas and everyone in the Federation are required to learn the English language. Because the Federation declared it as its universal language, it just makes sense for most leaders of other races and planets to learn English, too—at least well enough to communicate with the Federation.

Thanks to this, I think perhaps I can negotiate my way out of a painful death. After all, the Uuziks believe me to be part of the Federation Forces, which I'm certainly not. So there is a chance for my survival. I hope.

But I'm not about to walk into a firing line without some assurance.

"Tell your men to put down their weapons," I yell back, still shielding myself on the other side of the carrier ship.

Thanks to the heat sensors of my visor, I can see the enemies clearly, even if they're just red silhouettes. And, strangely enough, I can also hear guns being placed on the metal floor. They're listening to me. But why? Is it a trap? It has to be a trap—there's no way they'll talk peacefully with me. I know I said maybe there was a chance, but even I didn't believe that.

"You have my word—our weapons are down. Now please grant me the courtesy of seeing the dog who killed so many of my men," the tyrant says in a far more civil voice, one I didn't think Uuziks were capable of. This certainly wasn't the same way he talked to his underlings.

My mind is still running through and rejecting various plans as I stand from my crouched position and walk out. I have my gun ready and am aiming downward. There's no way I'm about to drop my guard until I know I'm safe.

But when I walk out, all the Uuziks' guns are indeed placed on the ground. There are 12 Uuzik underlings, and towering over them in the middle is the black and red scaled monster with its ugly prehistoric head.

My visor runs a quick scan to see if I can gather any info that might be helpful in my negotiations.

------------------------------------- Fenrich Valvatorez: Uuzik

**Fenrich is the highest-ranking official in the Uuzik hierarchy. He is listed as one of the top five most-wanted criminals in the Space Federation's data base for his over 430 counts of genocide, smuggling of goods, selling of planets, etc. With strength being the highest-regarded quality in Uuzik culture his rise up the ranks has come at the expense of many others' blood, including that of his own kind. If encountered, call the SFF immediately and do not engage.**

**Threat Level: Five stars ----------------------------------------**

At the end of the info is a list of crimes registered in the database. They're grouped together, but range from murders of important political figures on various planets to holding planets hostage and selling them for profit.

The last thing I want is to be part of his list of crimes, but considering how at odds myself and the Federation are, they might look the other way on this one.

Of course, if I manage to kill this brute, they might look the other way as well. Is killing a vaunted criminal illegal? Well yes, I'm pretty sure it still is. But as a mercenary, it's not that simple.

None of that matters right now, though—I just need to focus on saving my own life, a task that will not be easy.

Fenrich begins to speak. "So, what do we have here? A Federation dog sneaking around our base? No, that's not it. You don't don their garb. That is a suit unique to you, is it not? Who are you? Who do you work for?"

The tyrant points the sharp black scythe jetting out of his arm toward me, then steps forward through the crowd to the front. I instinctually shuffle backwards—the more distance between the two of us, the better.

"I'm just a sell star merc. I was sent to this planet on an exploration expedition," I lie. The last thing I'm willing to mention is anything about Calax Crystals. That would be a death wish.

The monster's hollowed eyes glare at me, examining my suit again.

"I see. Then allow me another question."

"And what would that be?"

"If what you say is true, and you come here only for exploration, then why break into our base? Why kill my hard-working men? Surely you have no reason to do all this if you're only here as a lowly sell star, no?"

I could tell the tyrant isn't buying my story, but for his next question, I can give him a more honest answer.

"You didn't exactly leave me with a lot of options, since you took the liberty of ravaging—not to mention blowing up—my ship and stranding me on this rock." The words come out with more vitriol than I expect, and I take an internal breath to calm myself. Raising my voice in a negotiation with these creeps will accomplish nothing.

"The only reason I came here is to look for a ship so I can get off this planet. Your men have not exactly been playing nice with me, though." I consider bringing up Project BB and bleeding out some information, but it seems like I'd be playing with my life due to the sensitivity of the details. That can be dealt with by the Federation—after my escape.

"Ahh, yes—the ship in the forest. It was quite the high-tech piece of technology from what our scientists could tell. May I ask who designed it?"

Now my suspicions are at their peak.

"Why?"

"The intricacies of the ship were intriguing. That sort of technology would help serve the Uuziks greatly."

I know my ship is a one-of-a-kind technology, like my suit, and this isn't the first time someone's asked me about it. Even a few different lifeforms throughout the years have asked if I would ever consider parting with it, to which the answer is and always will be no. However, I can't help but feel like I'd be putting the entire Bacardi race in danger with a truthful answer. They'd receive the same fate as my planet, and not only would it be my fault, but it would kill my best business partner as well.

"Sorry to disappoint, but I bought it off a drifter years ago," I brazenly lie again. "I don't know who made it."

Fenrich lets out a disgruntled sigh. "Why do humans always insist on lying about their accomplishments? They refuse to help others no matter the circumstances. We of the Uuziks do not care for your dishonesty. We decide everything based on strength. Those that are strong will always rise to the top of the pack. That is why the Federation, and people like you, must go. You continue to stifle growth by protecting the weaklings that do nothing more than take up precious resources. Power is what the universe revolves around. So with that in mind, allow me to make you a proposition in the way of our customs. How about we duel for the knowledge instead? If you can beat me in a battle of strength, I will grant you your freedom. You can take any of the ships here and be on your way. But if I win, then you will tell me all that I want to know about that ship."

"And how do I know you won't have your men interfere in this duel?"

"Because if they do, I'll kill them." His tone sends silent shocks through his men, I can tell. None of them look interested in getting involved, so I figure he's being honest.

But still I hesitate. Something about this opportunity seems too good to be true. I can get revenge on the monster who destroyed my planet, and be granted my freedom as well. Surely they understand the first thing I'd do is go to the SFF and inform them of my findings. Yet Fenrich shows no signs of worry. Not even for a moment does he believe he'll lose. That alone would be enough to put fear into any sane person, but, then again, sane people don't become mercenaries. Besides, it's not like I have the option to turn him down. He'd just kill me on the spot. So I swallow my anxiety and nod.

"Deal."

Fenrich reaches around his back and unsheathes a massive steel axe that attaches onto his scythe-like hands. He grips it with both arms, and the silver paint gleams in the sunlight.

I search his body, making sure no other weapons are concealed, but from what I can tell, nothing is hidden. The same can't be said for myself.

He brandishes the shining blade, pointing it at me with a grunt. One swing of that axe would cut my limbs clean off, armor or not. He rests the tip on the ground with a thud. Only the strongest of monsters could lift a hunk of metal that heavy, but, then again, I've already seen his power on display; he disposed of the threatening dorne-al without batting an eye. Compared to his weapon I'm walking around with a butter knife on my arm. But it's the best I have.

I let my blade jet out, and only then do I realize just how underprepared I am.

Fenrich storms toward me, leaving dents in the floor from his enormous strides. He lifts the blade high above his head and swings down with a vertical arc. My gut reaction is to block it with my blade, but my head thinks better of it. I jump out of the way, letting the axe crash down into the floor. When it does, I know I've made the right call. The axe shoots cracks throughout the floor's surface in all different directions. A few more swings and he could bring down the whole place. If I let that happen, we'd all be dead.

I get to my feet and dash forward, swinging my blade. If I can keep him from dictating the terms of our fight, perhaps I stand a chance.

Each slash clanks off his axe like I'm punching metal

with my fist. Not even a mark is left from my ten or so rapid and stealthy hacks.

As one would expect from a top-tier warrior of the Uuz-ik race, Fenrich is adept in his battle talents. He handles my ferocious swings with little effort, even when I think I can out-speed him. He defeats my best intentions of winning this battle at every turn. I'm way in over my head and beginning to see no way out.

I pause my pointless assault, and the tyrant grins at me mockingly.

"Is that the best you've got to offer, dog? You could come at me all day with those weak skills, and still you would never scratch me."

"I'm not done yet," I growl, feeling my blood boil at the monster who destroyed my planet, my family, my life.

I'm about to begin round two when the floor starts rumbling again. At first it's faint, but it gains intensity until parts of the ceiling are falling in.

But this time it can't be from Fenrich since he remains a few feet away from me.

I look around as do the Uuziks, trying to pinpoint the source of the noise.

Then, as if I'm beginning to hallucinate, I feel my legs start slipping backwards. The circular floor that's fashioned like an arena begins to tilt to the left.

It's not my imagination. The floor is tilting.

I and all the Uuziks standing across from me turn our attentions to the bizarre oddity before us.

A scaly hand with thin bones but jagged like sharp rocks grips the edge of the floor. Then a second hand shoots up, like a monster crawling up from under a bed.

The grip of this thing slips, and sparks shoot off in all directions as it struggles to regain its stranglehold on the ledge. It scrapes its claws before letting out a screech that shakes everyone in the room to their very core. A high-pitched cry shatters the glass roof above us. I still have no clue what fresh slice of hell is coming for me, but now I have tens of thousands of shattered glass shards falling toward me like knives.

I react first, diving underneath one of the large, arched ship wings, hearing the deafening machine gun fire of glass all around me. I hear Uuziks scrambling to grab their weapons again, along with a few screaming in pain as the shrapnel impales them.

I would've been in big trouble, but the now-armed Uuziks have no interest in me, at least for the time being. They're too busy dealing with our new threat.

Since I'm covered from the ship's wing, I sheath my blade and reach for my pistol in response. Another scream shrieks out, followed by a flash of something that shoots up into the sky and blocks out the sun. My back is pressed up against the ship's door, and I wonder if now is the time to escape. I don't think it'll work.

When I look around the wing, I can see the stomach of the beast. It looks boney and ancient, as if the skin has been burned clean off its body.

This is no miracle of life, but an abomination of science. And one that's set for battle.

It comes crashing down on the lip of the ledge, looking like a hybrid of a gigantic dorneal and an ancient dragon.

For having such a skeletal exterior, the monsters ferocious landing sounds like a boulder dropping.

Thanks to my hiding spot, I'm now in between this terrifying thing and the Uuziks. Not a good place to be.

Nonetheless, when I examine the beast, I notice something interesting.

It has patches of snow-white fur on its skin, and even the same shaped eyes as the treklet I saw before, only these are far more menacing.

Is this the bio-genetic creation that they've been designing with samples of different lifeforms? A combination of Calax Crystal and creatures just like the treklet, except far more dangerous?

Frozen in my own shock, I almost forget I have another problem just a few feet behind me. There are still numerous armed guards and a vicious tyrant that want my head.

On the bright side, I'm not their biggest problem, which gives me at least a shred of hope.

The Uuzik militia start to hail shots toward their own creation, while Fenrich starts to bark orders in his native tongue.

I wonder if this is their finished version of Project BB. Because if it is, that's a horrifying thought, but also, they seem to have no qualms about trying to kill it. That alone makes me think it must be another failed experiment.

I give the beast a quick scan hoping for some more information.

-------------------------------------------------------??? – ???:
-------------------------------------------------------- ????????

Now that is a new anomaly for me. My visor has never come back with zero information.

The mutated dragon starts to roar and growl as its body lights up with each shot fired, but the weapons are having no visible effect.

I decide to hop into the fray and fire off rounds as well, but even my well-placed blasts to the face and open rib cage land with a whimper.

After a while, the beast has smoke rising off its skeletal body, but this only makes it angrier. It lets out a battle cry and takes its long tail with a triangular tip and cuts through the air. Of course, my head is its first target.

I use my thrusters to spring up, getting out of there as quickly as I can, but the collateral damage is done.

I look down from my aerial view and get a clear image of the horrible destruction below me. The monster's tail rips through the ship that was once my hiding spot and then swings it into a few other ships, sending them all toppling over the edge in an avalanche of destruction. My hopes of escape are whisked away like evening trash, down the chute of the base and never to be seen from again.

A fall from that height will ensure the ships are wrecked beyond repair. But, more importantly at this moment, now I have no cover for myself.

I hover in the air for a couple of seconds, trying not to shed a tear for my lost hopes. I'm now truly at the mercy of the Uuziks and whatever this thing is that's on the verge of making the Uuziks—or my escape— irrelevant.

While I hang in the air, suspending disbelief at my own luck, a giant claw swipes at me like the grim reaper swinging a scythe. I throw my body to the left hoping and literally praying that my thrusters won't give out.

The tip of its jagged rock-like claw scrapes the edge of my suit leaving a sullied mark, but I avoid any major damage. But before I can make a second move, the monster charges at me, palming my face with its other claw.

I can feel my suit's helmet and backplate compressing like a can of beans about to explode. All I can see through my visor are the yellow-stained bones of the monster as it takes me for a hellish joy ride. And if it isn't clear: joy for him, hell for me.

Before I know what's happening, the beast smashes me along the wall of the dome and flies forward, dragging me with it. Sparks light up my visor while my ears bleed from the cries of screeching metal on metal.

It would be nice for the Uuziks to step in right about now, but of course they don't care if I'm the one killed by their own creation. It's only serving its purpose.

Once my rollercoaster ride comes to an end, the beast finishes by slamming me down in a way that I'm sure make the Uuziks proud.

I hit the floor so hard that I bounce half my height before falling to a crippled stop. I try to open my eyes, but every nerve in my body screams. Even the slightest movement is too much of an effort.

Then a strange pressure begins applying itself on my body, like my suit is compressing in on me. But it isn't a malfunction of my suit—it's the monster's boney foot pinning me down like spikes.

I have no strength left in my body to fight it. I'm sure at this point I look like a pile of scrap metal. My visor has cracks in it like shattered ice, and if it breaks outright, my oxygen will cease to function. This, clearly, will only add to my problems.

With my head sticking out from between the gnarled toes of the beast, I watch it lift its knife-like fingers up and prepare to slice me like a guillotine.

Throughout my years of tumultuous adventures, I've gone up against so many different monsters and lifeforms that've posed various threat levels. Some even had me bested, and should've had me dead to rights, but nothing's made me shutter at the prospect of death quite like this thing.

As a merc, you know death can be around any corner, but in no way am I ready to die.

I don't know where the strength inside me is coming from, but something in my heart refuses defeat to this grotesque monster, and certainly not a creation from those who wiped out my planet.

Pain still ripping through my arms (luckily, my legs have lost feeling), I know I need to come up with a plan. Thankfully my arms are still functional, because they're all I need.

The Uuziks continue to rain fire on the beast enough to just mildly irritate it. I would kill for the power hungry Fenrich to step in and lend me a hand, but it seems he has more interest in seeing how I handle this situation. And I refuse to disappoint.

In the face of impending death, a plan finally comes to mind. Not a great one, I'll admit, but the only one that could possibly work.

But none of it will come to fruition if not for a small miracle first, and, from all things, an Uuzik solider.

One of the Uuziks' blasts hits a small tuft of fur on the monster's elbow joint, causing it to let out a bloodcurdling scream.

More importantly, the shot is enough to make the unidentifiable monster's guillotine thrust downward just an inch to my left instead of my head. The pressure of its foot lifts from my torso only for a second, but that's more than enough space for me to contort my body. I have one hope, and only one hope.

If Calax Crystals are the reason I'm in this mess, then they'll be the thing that gets me out of it.

I grab my pistol with my left hand. With my right, I curl my fingers to tap the button on my suit, which opens my arm compartment. The stash where I'm keeping my Calax Crystals opens, and I shake one loose onto the ground. It gleams in the sun as it rolls toward my face. Palpable energy radiates off the gem, giving me a glimmer of hope.

That said, in the back of my mind, I'm still worried about pissing the Uuziks off further, but they have bigger problems to deal with—and so do I. Hopefully, they're too preoccupied with the personification of death pinning everyone down.

I pop open the small hatch on the bottom of my blaster and let the tiny orange crystal fall out. It's a rather common mineral—Descox—that anyone can find in the caves of TOTI-3, which is an icy tundra of a planet. They're so abundant and versatile that almost every modern-day weapon is powered by it. Mine still has a heavy glow, which means almost none of its energy reserve has been depleted, mainly because I replaced it before starting this mission. It won't pack near enough punch though, so I stash it away for later and jam the Calax Crystal into my blaster. The insane and wildly dangerous resource wastes no time filling my pistol with overwhelming energy. My blaster begins to turn red like magma.

For all I know, the abundance of energy will melt my pistol into a useless pile of mush, but between that and waiting for death, I have to take my chances.

Twisting my body as much as I can, I aim my gun upward. I wish I could say it's a perfectly aimed shot, one I've practiced day in and day out for this very moment, but the truth is that I aim with blind hope. What can I say, though—sometimes things just work out.

One shot—that's all it takes. A red and yellow beam explodes from the barrel like a giant laser. The force nearly puts me through the floor for good, but that'll be getting off easy compared to the skeletal dragon beast.

The beam rips through the jaw of the dragon and up through his head. The power of my Calax Crystal doesn't stop there, though; it blows though the monster's jaw and straight into the sky and beyond.

Not only am I in shock with this scope of power, but I'm pretty sure all the Uuziks are, too.

It makes me wonder: Why aren't they using this sort of energy in their weapons? I mean, they have thousands upon thousands of these energy sources on hand.

But I get my answer when I try to fire my second shot.

My blaster stalls.

While the agonizing cries of a dragon with a hole through its jaw bellow out, I slam my pistol off the ground in another act of blind hope. Only this time, it doesn't work.

Instead, as it hits the dented floor, the pistol breaks

apart, melting away like goo. I curse under my breath, but if I only had one bullet in the chamber, at least I made it count.

Then, in a blur, I see the tyrant Fenrich leap high into the air. It's hard to see through my heavily damaged mask, but I can definitely hear the sound of his axe swinging and breaking the bony exterior of the beast. It cries out again, this time with less energy as its life begins to fade.

The beast splits in two, falling lifelessly in half. It tumbles backwards, careening over the ledge and down into the abyss where it'll join the half a dozen ships that most likely lay in pieces alongside it.

At first, I can't be more thankful to be free from this monster's clutches, but then something else occurs to me: I was right—there's no way that thing was the vaunted Project BB. My earlier theory revolved around them not choosing to dispose of something they worked so hard to create. But now, I think I'm wrong.

I'm not saying the Uuziks wouldn't kill their own creation; what I mean is that if they planned on using that thing to take on the Federation, it would have needed to be a hundred times stronger.

Now I wonder if it was some sort of prototype, or just a botched experiment like the devil treklet? I can't be sure, but for the time being, those questions don't matter. I have a much bigger issue on my hands.

The landing thud of the Uuzik leader lifts my broken body off the ground, but even this can't convince me to rise to my feet. Through the cracks in my visor, I can only see the awkwardly shaped feet of Fenrich walking up to me.

He puts his claw-like toes on my chest, pressing down on me as he speaks.

"So…you were hiding Calax Crystals in that suit of yours. And let me guess—you were planning to use it in a pinch during a fight. You dog. How stupid do you think I am, trying to pass yourself off as some explorer…"

He kicks me viciously in the ribs, sending me flipping over a few times before landing with a thud near the edge of the dome. I must be only a foot or two away from where the botched experiment fell to its death just moments earlier.

Fenrich walks over and picks me up by the arm, holding me in mid-air like a limp piece of rope. All I can do is dangle back and forth. My body is well past the point of being able to scream; in fact, I'm not sure I even have any voice left.

"You're strong, and I respect the courage it takes to stand against me in battle, even when you knew you would lose. Unfortunately, that appears to have worked against you in this situation."

I want to speak. I think I even move my lips in an effort to say "hold on," but nothing comes out.

"Staying silent in the face of death, I see."

"Look," I finally manage to spit out. "I just want off this planet. I hate the Federation as much as you do. I have no business with you or the Uuzik race."

I try to speak firmly since I know that any form of begging or weakness will only get me killed faster. But I also refuse to cower in front of these monsters. I won't give them the satisfaction.

"If I were you, I wouldn't worry about getting off this

planet. I'd just worry about surviving your next fall. Do that, and maybe I will grant you your freedom."

I can already see the scene playing out in my mind before it happens, but whatever I imagine, the real thing will be infinitely worse. I peek through my almost closed eyes. I can see the grotesque yet sinister smile of a monster, all too proud of what he's about to do.

A cold shiver runs down my spine, but before I can react, he tosses me like a rag doll. I hear a menacing laugh fading out of range as I began to plummet like a missile into the abyss below.

MANY BAD THINGS CAN HAPPEN AS A MERCENARY. In fact, really only a few good things can happen, and that's if the missions go exactly as planned. This is not one of those times.

The base's cylinder-like structure has either been built for one of two reasons as far as I can see it. Either they envisioned the sick intent of tossing people overboard to their death or…nope, never mind—that's the only reason I can think of as to why they'd build it this way.

As I plummet to my impending date with death, all I can see are walls of metal and stone whizzing past me.

Let me tell you something: When you're falling from an unholy height and you don't know when you'll hit the bottom, that's almost as sobering a thought as actually falling. After all, it's not the fall itself that kills you—it's the sudden stop at the end of it.

I have a plan, though. Today will not be the day I freefall to my demise. After all, I still have unfinished business with those Uuzik scum, and now I want revenge more than ever.

But, of course, I need to take things one step at a time here. Even in a freefall, the key to survival as a mercenary is thinking logically and concisely. No wasted seconds.

I did luck out in one regard, though. Either through neglect or arrogance, Fenrich dropped me sailing down legs first, which is a huge advantage.

I activate my thrusters to full strength, just like when I was plummeting down the cliff after the dorneal. Only this time, I have more power on my side.

After seeing the power of Calax Crystals firsthand in my pistol, I assume the same effects can be applied to my suit as well.

I grip my arm compartment tight as I detach the casing. One crystal hits the top of my hand as I try to hold the others at bay.

Thankfully, my thrusters are strong enough to slow my decent, allowing me to pull off the precise maneuver, but the problem is that they'll only last a few seconds. And when they turn, it's all over.

There are also no doors or alcoves that I can try to steer in with my reduced speed. I whip past the upper three floors in seconds, leaving me with no hope of landing on the bridges, either. I hadn't thought of that idea quick enough.

With the power source in hand, I hold it to the center of my chest, where a small battery compartment is located. The second it pops open, the power source inside springs out and flies up above me. I jam the new power into my chest and slam the door shut, just in time for my thrusters to kick off.

Now I'm in real trouble, and I have no way of knowing how much runway I have for this plan to work. Could be 30 seconds, maybe 15…or I could be dead before I blink my eyes next. I have no way of knowing.

These two to three seconds during which I have no thrusters—and also no clue if I'll abruptly smash into the ground with a splatter—are easily in the top five scariest things to happen to me in this line of work.

Once the Calax Crystal is stuffed in my suit chest, all I can do is close my eyes and let the radiating heat course through my body. Just like my gun heating up to the point of boiling, my suit and body are doing the same. My blood starts to pump faster and my head starts to become fuzzy, making me wonder if I've made a horrible mistake. My suit isn't designed for such explosive power, and if it goes the same route as my melted blaster…well, I don't think I need to paint that image for you.

But my other choice is death, so my options aren't exactly at a premium.

A painful yet wonderful jolt grabs at my body, trying to rip me out of my suit. My thrusters kick back on just as I'd hoped, and with the power of the crystals, they increase in power two if not threefold. My speed reduces drastically, but I'm quickly running out of time.

In all honesty, this fall must be no more than 20…maybe 25 seconds of my life at most—and, granted, that is an eternity for a fall—but in this moment, it feels like minutes, if not hours.

I come to a screeching halt, and through the shine of my

thrusters I begin to see the floor. Gravity practically rips me out of my suit as I reach the impact site.

Crash.

I hit the ground, going into a tuck and roll to brace myself. I bounce off the pavement and smash into a wall, my mask filled with broken glass, blood, and gravel.

Blackness ensues.


Drip, drip, drip…

Small blots of sewage water drop down in perfect intervals, working their way to creating a puddle. The stone plane of the inner planet refuses to soak up any water, and it's also as hard as anything the universe has to offer. Of course, I might be a bit biased saying that, because when I smash off the bedrock, nothing could feel harder.

But the water isn't what wakes me up from my unconscious slumber. It's the sound of scurrying rat-like creatures that snaps my eyes open.

One of them with rough, grey fur sits on its hindlegs, staring at me with beady black eyes. For a moment, it bears its tiny fangs at me, but once I roll over the little creature runs away frightened.

After my eyes open and the blurry vision of an abrupt wake-up call fades, all I can make out are black and gray looking rocks, and the occasional flash of a water droplets making their way from a pipe to the ground before exploding on impact. I feet its pain.

"Ugh…" The excruciating pain of falling an ungodly distance is on full display. Then it occurs to me: Wait…I can feel pain…does that mean I survived? I can't believe such a hastily put-together plan worked. If I could drag my body up to a proper position, I'd celebrate my success. But as it stands, I'm glued to the ground.

This pain feels different, though. It's as if my body is being ripped apart at the seams. My blood feels hot…well past healthy temperatures, and I have a funny feeling I knew why. Obviously I had no choice, but in using Calax Crystals to survive, chances are it'll carry some consequences for having such power so close to my body. The effects on my body now are ruthless, but I can only hope that's all it'll be. Who knows what long-term issues could arise. But, again, I have little say in the matter. Besides, the price I'm currently paying is still pennies compared to the price my suit will pay.

I don't need an outside view to know the damage report. My prized possession has suffered dents, scrapes, chips, and outright broken parts all at once.

Finally, I push myself to one knee, taking a look through my severely cracked visor. Another lucky break, I suppose. My helmet only sustains fractures. Although massive in size, if my helmet broke entirely, my survival plan would've been a waste of time anyways. It's still pumping oxygen into my body. Wait…my oxygen. Honestly, for a moment I forget all about that fairly significant detail.

My life has been threatened so many different times in such a short span that even surviving 24 hours on this cursed planet seems like the least of my concerns.

Fearful of how much time I lost while unconscious, I tap my helmet, detecting chips of rock and gravel jammed in along the cracks. I run my finger until I find the sensor, and then I tap it.

Nothing.

The counter refuses to show.

That's a big problem, and one that will stretch well beyond suffocation. It means that my suit has lost power. When I added the overflowing energy of the Calax Crystal, I hastily ejected my battery supply.

Just as with my pistol, in which the crystal dissolved after being drained of its energy, so too did the crystal in my suit. It's left me powerless.

That doesn't directly affect my oxygen supply, thank God, because the Bacardi are better engineers than that. But as for every other function my suit provides me, I'm currently out of luck.

Still, acting on impulse or panicking will only get me killed faster. It's one thing to die from lack of oxygen, and even though I have no clue when that might happen, it's out of my control. Dying because of something I have no control over isn't worth worrying about.

The first step in my escape is to evaluate my situation. Since I've dropped about a million miles underground, the most I can gather is that I'm still in the Uuzik base, at least in some way or another.

Also, I'm in a dead-end sewage pit. There are more than a few dead bodies splattered around me on the ground, most of which are, surprisingly, Uuziks. There are other different looking species as well, but with their bodies in such a mangled state, I can't make out where they came from. And, of course, the ships, though most of them are shattered beyond repair.

The last thing I spot are the twisted bodies of some dead animals. Failed experiments, I assume. But the one thing I'm most surprised to not find is the dead body of that skeletal dragon-like beast. Could it have lived and made an escape…or did something else happen to it? For the time being, it doesn't matter, I suppose.

Since my suit can't function, my path isn't exactly clear, so I start flipping pieces of scrap metal out of my way. I honestly can't tell you why. I'm just desperate and looking for anything that might help.

I continue to dig through the scrap, but I stop when I stumble upon something strange. A hand…a human hand, cold and white. The only saving grace in finding the hand is that it isn't severed; I pull off another scrap of ship metal and find the rest of the cold body slouched over, lifeless.

The man, who looks like an Earthling, is wearing a uniform—one that belongs to the Federation. It's the same blue and red button-up uniform, though the colours are faded now. It's clear he wasn't treated to the same cliff-diving excitement that everything else down here fell prey to. This is entirely evident due to a streak of blood that stretches down from the left side of his chest along his uniform and into a small puddle on the ground. An obvious bullet wound.

I guess I can count my lucky stars that the Uuziks didn't kill me when they had the opportunity. At least they gave me the chance to survive.

I walk up to the poor, lifeless soul and pop the cracked, red helmet off his head. It's a more rounded, traditional style than mine. The man's skin hasn't started decaying, but his eyes are glossed over with a blank stare. Based on his condition, I assume this man must have died fairly recently. But seeing a Fed solider down here makes me wonder: Does this mean the Federation is on to the Uuz-iks? Is that why the Uuziks assumed I was one of them so quickly? It would make some sense considering the Uuz-iks' clear level of paranoia.

But if the Federation Forces are investigating already, then why haven't they sent more troops, a full army even? There are a lot of dead bodies around here, but only one in a Federation uniform. The others just look like unfortunate travelers.

Unsure of the answers, I put the questions aside. Then I pause for a moment. I don't know why, but I give a silent prayer for those that have fallen before me. I place my hand over my chest and close my eyes.

After this moment of silence, a thought occurs to me and I snap my eyes open.

*Come on…come on, come on. Be in here.* I start to pat the dead body down, in search of a specific object. Not finding what I want in the front pockets, I reach around to the back. Part of me is admittedly concerned that this crypt-like body will spring to life and hug me in return. Obviously, it doesn't do any such thing, but rummaging through the pockets of dead bodies is something I've never been a fan of.

I reach into his back pocket and grab something matching the shape of what I'm looking for, and I pull it out and examine it. The object is a small blue rectangle that fits inside my palms. In the middle of this hunk of metal is a small black button that takes up most of the surface area, and along the bottom are five smaller buttons numbered accordingly.

The device is a distress signal given to every Federation

trooper for emergency use. The black light would be blue if the trooper had activated it, but evidently, he was never given that chance.

And, of course, the Federation would never bother to check on a ground trooper unless the beacon is activated. If you don't get a chance to activate your distress call and are killed, then they don't care to double check. That might be a harsh perspective on the Federation's upper captains, but I know for some of them it's 100% true. I give the beacon a second look, checking the back to see if it's been broken or damaged in any way. Amazingly, it's in perfect condition.

I tap the black button and it lights up blue. Then I punch in a five-digit code that I remember from my Federation days and hit the big now-glowing button again. Then, just like my hopes, the light fades and the device shut off.

*Don't tell me the battery is dead on this thing.* I follow the same steps again, which results in the same blinking light that fades into nothing. Wait…it probably can't get a signal while I'm so far underground. Unbelievable all the technology the Federation has, and they can't get a bloody beacon that works underground.

I'll admit that there's a bit of ego involved when the button's light fades again. Like I said earlier, thinking with a clear rational mind is key. In the moment, though, I want to smash this little box against the wall for being such a cheap piece of junk.

But it's more than that. It's about needing the help of the Federation to survive, something I swore to myself I would never let happen when I made the choice to go solo.

Options are sparse though, and pride would be the final

nail in my coffin. So I have no choice — I need to get to the surface, use the distress signal, and rest my hopes on the Federation that's let me down so many times in the past.

But any way I slice it, I need to get moving. Not before I deal with the biggest issue at hand, though. Since I overloaded my suit and it now ceases to function, I know that fixing it is my top priority.

I look around. My best bet lies in the numerous ships that tumbled to their deaths with me. Although if I hadn't previously known what they were, I never would've been able to tell they were ships. It's still my only chance. I just have to pray that one has power.

Digging through the scrap pile proves to be nothing more than an exercise in futility. As would be getting into most of the cockpits, since the roofs are caved in so badly.

The ones that pass as structurally sound have no power, and no materials or supplies that would be helpful. I walk up to the last of the six ships, my hopes fading. I step up onto the metal wing of the downed bird and start to peel off chunks of metal.

With the way the ship landed, the long, curved wing folded in on itself, blocking the cockpit. Luckily, it's cushioned the impact enough to keep the machine intact. I drop my full body weight onto the metal sheet, breaking part of it off. I toss the scrap out of my way and crawl headfirst into the tight pilot seat.

As you'd expect, the inside of the ship hasn't stood up well. The controls are smashed, and loose wires are hanging everywhere, giving off sparks. Sparks! That's when an incredibly stupid, but also completely plausible plan forms in my head.

What if I can jump start my suit's power with the sparks coming from these cables? If I can get my emergency back-up battery fired up, then if nothing else, I'll get my visor back online. With that, I'll be back in business. At least in some respect.

But before I can do anything, I need to create a bigger opening.

After crawling back out, I look for any more metal I can peel off. Even though my body wants to give out with each step, I grab the top of the metal fold and let my feet go limp. The structure has enough damage that bending it back to the point of breaking shouldn't be hard. I hang off the metal ledge and let my bodyweight do most of the work.

I can feel it bend in half as my back slowly descends down to the floor. Then, just to add minor insult to injury, I hear the metal flap finally snap. Then my suspension in the air gives out, landing me hard on my back. I cough up my precious oxygen and groan as loud as I can. Just another bruise in an already horrific day.

At least when I push the metal sheet off my bartered body, I can confirm I've accomplished exactly what I'd hoped for: A much clearer path is created, and one I can actually stand up in.

But now I need to test to see if any of my hard work will bear fruit. With any luck, those sparks will have enough juice. I'll still have no pistol, but to have access to my scanner once again—not to mention my map—would be more than enough to make up for my lack of protection.

I grab the wires, one being red and the other one blue. Now comes the tricky part. The backup battery in my suit isn't located in my chest like the original was; it's in the back of my helmet, which makes inserting the wires rather difficult. I've complained to the Bacardi about changing it many times in the past, which obviously fell on deaf ears. For such a technologically advanced species, they're rather stubborn about their designs.

But I guess I could ration the logic, in a sense. If I'd managed to land hard enough to damage that backup battery in my helmet, chances are I would've been killed anyways, so it wouldn't have been an issue.

I touch the wires together gently, trying to avoid sending sparks firing toward me. A good shock might not kill me, but with the little strength remaining in my body, there's the chance I might black out from it. And if that happens, by the time I wake up…no, scratch that. I won't wake up because I'm sure I'll be out of oxygen.

Taking the red cable on the left, I place it into one of the small slots on the back of my helmet. A jolt surges through my body, but thankfully it's nothing more than the small shock you'd get from generating a bit of static on a carpet. The blue one plugs in next, and another shock courses into my body. If I wasn't awake before, I sure am now.

Faint beeping swirls through my ears, and then a flicker in front of my eyes blinds me. Seeing stars for a moment, words begin to scroll up my screen like a computer booting up. A bunch of jargon flies past my eyes in rapid succession, not that I need to read these bootup instructions; if something isn't working, it always appears in bold red text. But there's none of that, and my suit continues a full scan of itself. Now I'm in business. Ninety seconds later, all my usual functions return, and so the first thing I do is check my oxygen timer.

4:57.

Phew, I still have a little bit of time. I also still have a chance.

Exhaling a small breath of victory, the next step is pulling up the map data I snagged right before everything went to hell.

The 3D map beams out in front of me, and I zoom in before spinning to get a clearer view of my location.

Bingo. The orange dot at the bottom of the spiraling tower confirms my location.

I knew I'd been tossed a long way, but now I can confirm I've hit rock bottom—literal rock bottom.

But when I spin the map around again, a brief opening to an even further tunnel that looks like an elevator shaft catches my eye. I speculate that it leads even further into the planet's core, which is curious. Why would they continue building all the way down to the planet's core? Is it possible they'd mined so much Calax Crystal that they were required to go deeper into the planets depths to find more? No, that can't be it—I found crystals easily and I remember seeing many different veins on the map. Perhaps…no, for sure they're hiding something down there. I just don't know what.

As much as exploring deeper could answer those questions, with no blaster and no time, I simply can't add that to my growing list of problems.

I flick the map off and set out. With a functional suit, at least I'm in business. I also now have a distress beacon at my disposal. If nothing else, I want to get back to the surface and make sure that the beacon activates. If I'm to die in the process, I can at least screw over the

Uuziks one last time…if the Federation doesn't go and screw it up first.

Because of where I've landed, there's only one logical path I can take. Based on my map, I label my location as the level two basement—before I can get to the main floor of the tower, there's another floor above me that I'll have to get past.

This trek won't be nearly as far as the first one, and I figure it's safe to say the Uuziks won't be on high alert. Actually, I'm quite sure of that. The Uuziks and Fenrich figure me to be dead.

But despite all my attempts to convince them I'm not part of the Federation, they refuse to buy it. Because of this, if I put my thought process into the mind of the war-hungry monsters, then I'd expect more Federation soldiers to arrive soon once they realize one of their men have been killed.

Obviously I know this isn't the case, but since they already killed one, and then (so they think) a second one (me) they could assume war is on the horizon when showing up.

The first path I follow has a bend like most of the rest of the building due to its circular nature. The walls are bedrock stone, and the ground is a mix between dirt and rock.

With each cautious step forward, I keep one eye planted on my map and the other right in front of me. My ears are also at the ready, expecting to hear any slight sound that would alert me of other life that may be around.

But I hear nothing except for small drops of water reverberating off the walls, as well as my own trepidatious footsteps.

I go all the way around the bend until I reach the end. A large metal door, looking far more secure than any of the upper base doors, blocks my path. Except it doesn't. In fact, it's wide open.

My instincts obviously make me question this, but I can't be bothered. It's either a careless mistake or I'm being bated into a trap. Either way, I'm going through.

I cautiously step into the room and take a look around. I'm still stuck in the pits of the tower, but at least my new location has a more modern-base feel to it, and not that of a dumpster crater.

This room, and presumably all rooms moving forward, is a man-made base. Or an Uuzik-made base. I'm still not sure how they've pulled all this off.

This room reminds me of the second-floor terrarium room, only the atmosphere is far less luscious. Actually, there's not much atmosphere to speak of at all. I'm in another lab, this one with lines and lines of tubes and containers, some big enough to accommodate an animal twice my size.

This must be where they do the infusions with the Calax Crystals. They probably keep them here until ready to be placed in the second-floor terrarium for growth.

Each of the oversized tubes hold a different exotic-looking creature in them, most of which I've never seen before.

I walk up to a group of three smaller-than-average canisters. Inside are three little treklets, babies perhaps, floating up and down in the murky green liquid that fills the jars. These creatures are curled up in the sleeping position, but they look a bit more like their brethren from official pictures rather than the mutant monster — which, by the way, is still on the loose.

After I skip past a few more odd-looking creatures, I come across one that piques my interest. In a far bigger jar than the one that houses the treklets floats a four-legged creature with bright orange and brown fur, and a yellow mane that flows down its back toward its thin, waving tail. I give the creature a quick scan, glad to have my visor back online.

---------------------------------- **Leijor: Lion family, Male**

**Leijor are rare creatures found on the Indigo forests of DM-32. Primarily known as hunting creatures, the leijors like to run in packs, but the leader likes to stay behind and watch as his tribe hunts. Leijors have a thick mane that spreads across their body, allowing them to keep warm in the cooler climates of their home planet.**

**Threat Level: Three Stars** ---------------------------------------

Once I learn that the creature is a leijor, it suddenly becomes more recognizable to me. The report mentioning DM-32 helps jog my memory a bit, too.

A few years ago when I was still kicking around the Federation, I spent more than a month on DM-32. To this day, that planet is the coldest place I've ever been to. Each minute of every day, our crew was begging to be given the okay to leave.

Memories of those days are fuzzy at best. I do remember us coming across a pack of leijors strutting around, though.

We made sure to stay as far away as possible. Our commander made it clear that leijors will never hesitate to attack. How the Uuziks managed to tame one and get it back to this base was a feat of skill, but also one of insanity.

However just like the treklet, this leijor doesn't match the pictures on my visor, nor the brief memories I can recall. The leijors I knew were more an egg-white colour, with little steel accents in their manes. Is this another form of metamorphosis, too? I figure it must be. That, or the creature has managed to get quite the tan while being stuck on RG-87.

More questions come to mind about this creature, and, all the other creatures not native to this planet for that matter.

How the Uuziks are managing to transport wildlife under the noses of the Federation can only be a testament to the Feds' arrogance, but I still have to wonder why.

To me, the Uuziks are gathering creatures on both RG-87 as well as other planets across the universe and are running experiments on them. Calax Crystals, as I've seen numerous times now, take drastic and usually critical effects on everything they combine with. Do the Uuziks want to see which creatures can handle doses of Calax Crystals? No, that can't be it.

I think back to the skeletal dragon monster that helped foil my first escape. The beast had tufts of fur similar to that of the treklets, but it otherwise looked nothing like a treklet. But now I can see a little bit of a similarity between the beast's tail, and the leijor's. Obviously a longer skeletal version, but with the same strange, pointed tip.

The next creature I come across is a bird, but it's not a dorneal as one might expect. It's a tiny bird, one that could rest in the palm of my hand comfortably. It has a sea-blue star on its green, crested body. The star has a small glow to it, reminding me of when I'd jammed the Calax Crystal into my pistol.

**------------------------------ Cardinal: Bird family, Female**

**Cardinals live in heat-condensed areas like the planet JE–11, which is known for its blistering hot weather. Through evolution, the cardinal loses most of its feathers, creating an almost bone-like outline along its body.**

**Threat Level: Two Stars ----------------------------------------**

The pictures show a majestic bird far bigger than this little baby, with a massive wingspan and matching beautiful blue feathers lining the bottoms. It sort of looks like the skeletal dragon. The pieces of the puzzle are starting to fit. It's possible that the Uuziks are running experiments on individual creatures as well, but now I'm beyond confident about the reason they dragged these creatures here: They're creating an amalgamation of monsters in conjunction with Calax Crystals. Chances are that any creature on its own would turn out like the mutated treklet, so they must be combing creatures and trying to create a monster that can handle the power they want to grant it.

I take another look at the bird and its glowing chest. It might be too late for this little guy, unfortunately. It might be too late for all of them. I imagine they've all undergone the same Calax Crystal injections, which means that if they don't survive the effects, they'll be discarded.

Being sentimental will get me nowhere, though. As harsh as that reality is, they're just creatures, and although they never asked for this horrible fate, they're already lost. I'm not. And anyways, it's not like I can do much for them.

If I try to release them and they turn traitor to attack me, I'll be paying the price for my own stupidity. And I've had enough run-ins with these weird and horrific experiments as it is.

At the other end of the room is an elevator shaft, except its doors are missing.

Walking up to the edge of the shaft, flashbacks of falling to my death fill my mind as I look downward into the black void of nothing. Also, there's no elevator to be seen, and the buttons along the wall are colorless. When I tap the biggest one to call what I hope will be my ride, nothing happens. No green light, no sound, just more disappointment. Of course.

At this point, if there was any chance for me to get an easy ride out, it would obviously just be a myth. I mean, it would have been quite a shock if the Uuziks were so careless as to let me waltz on out by way of an elevator. Things rarely come so easy, especially when everyone on the planet is trying to kill you.

But at least it means nobody will be sneaking up on me.

Looking up again, I can see a faint orange light, far above my head—one of the stops leading me to the first-floor basement.

"Well, nowhere to go but up, I guess," I shrug, knowing I'll have to forge my own path forward.

But before I do that, I jump into the air a few times,

letting my hover pack do its work before landing with a small thud. The first thing I want to check is that my thrusters still work. Unlike my dead blaster, they've survived the influx of Calax Crystal energy. I guess my suit is a little more durable.

Second on my list is checking my legs. I need to know that despite their weakness that they can handle an abrupt landing. Short of jumping into the elevator shaft with blind faith, jumping up and down a few times is the best I can do. I stick my head back into the elevator shaft and look up again.

About thirty, maybe forty feet. That shouldn't be too bad. I look across from my spot and see a nice groove I can land on. It's maybe the size of my heel, but if I stand on my tiptoes, it'll be fine.

I take one final glance upward, this time to make sure that no elevator is coming. With the coast clear, I back up a few steps and take a deep breath. Compared to the many difficult stunts I've pulled off today, a few leaps and some well-timed thruster maneuvers should be nothing. Besides, I've undergone my fair share of unusual — if not downright evil — training in my Federation days.

Every day for nearly three years, I underwent vigorous, torturous training. I'd be forced to climb up metal ropes nearly twenty feet high, or crawl through fields of gravel and rock for kilometers at a time. And that's the easy stuff — it got much, much worse from there. And best of all? It was all tailored specifically for me because I was younger than all the others in the recruitment system.

When I say that I hated every minute of those days, I mean every minute, but the reason for this was because

I wasn't a recruit. I was nothing more than a small baby who watched his family and planet being slaughtered by a group of monsters. Despite surviving, I had nowhere to go, so I was taken away by a bunch of people from space. I never asked to join the Federation—it's not like it was some dream of mine. But at least it's coming in handy right about now.

I take off in a full sprint, ignoring that my legs feel like wooden pegs. Hitting the edge of the elevator shaft, I jump as far and as high as I can with my remaining strength.

The width of the elevator shaft is a little more than ten feet wide, so getting to the other wall isn't an issue. But the steps that come after is where my problems begin.

While mid-air, I use my thrusters to bump me up an extra foot or two before landing on the far ledge, my back pressed against the cold rock. I sidled to my left a tad to get into a better position. Like I said, the first jump was easy; I had a running start.

I look up even further and see the orange light of my destination glowing a bit brighter. Through the rusty gleam I can see ropes—wires, actually—dangling from the top of the shaft. I can climb all the way up it, and even skip the other floors if I'm lucky. But first I need to grumble a bit at the fact that my Federation training will be an asset. It's a tradition for me.

Crouching down into a power stance, I perform my best standing long jump and take a leap of faith. My thrusters once again add a small boost, and I grab the free-hanging rope praying that it's tethered to something tight.

Hand over hand, I pull myself up as I've done so many times in the past.

I hear a heavy, unfamiliar noise in the distance. It sounds like a train racing down the tracks, screeching metal on the rails. I pause, looking down below me, but I see nothing. I look up. Nothing but that faint orange glow.

Am I just being paranoid about the possibility of an elevator showing up? As it turns out—no. The sound increases in its intensity, and so does my anxiety. Soon the sound is as loud as a storming jet engine.

I know from most historical textbooks that when they show pictures of elevators, they're these slow-moving box-like rides that use a pulley system, but those have been out of date since teleportation took off in the 34th century. But in the time between those two developments, elevators used jet propulsions, similar to the thrusters in my suit. It wouldn't surprise me if the Bacardi invented this system, too.

I can see a white light above, beaming toward me. It grows rapidly, faster than I can react. I start to spin myself on the ropes, looking for a place to jump. Going backwards is not an option based on momentum, but staying still is begging for death.

Out of the corner of my eye, I spot a trim of metal similar to the one I stood on previously. But this one is about half the size of the other trim, which means that standing on it will be almost impossible. But it's not like I have time to question it; roars are upon me and I feel the heat from the propulsion jet baring down.

I use my momentum to swing the rope back and forth before taking a leap through the air. The elevator is only about three or four seconds away from me. I pray it doesn't take up the entire width of the shaft. If it does, I'm done for.

My forward momentum is weak, and I can tell I have no chance of making it as I sail through the air. I come up with one last-ditch effort. I stretch out as far as I can and activate my thrusters to provide an extra inch of height, grabbing onto the ledge with my fingertips. I dangle there, holding myself up with one arm, but by no more than a few fingers. My arm feels ready to detach at any moment as my limp body pulls it down.

The force heading down on me makes my already weighty, metal-covered body feel two or three times heavier.

Like a jet engine, the rectangular metal transport box flashes by me before I can blink. Ignoring my bleeding ears caused by the bombastic noise, the rush of air shoves my dangling chest against the wall, nearly forcing free my death grip on the metal rim.

But my grip tightens, and I refuse to give up. Summoning the refusal of death, I yank myself up, in part thanks to the boost of my thrusters taking some weight off me. I cling to the ledge with no room to move. One more good long jump, and then I grab the wires again. Maybe I can hitch a ride if the elevator comes back up.

Eventually, I get to the same height as the glowing orange light. This is exactly what I've been praying for, a door to the basement first floor. I launch myself again and clutch onto the nearby metal rim, pulling myself up. I choose to start on the opposite side of the vent and sidle my way around, rather than grabbing onto the door ledge and risk it opening with me in a precarious position. I maneuver my way around, one inch at a time. This narrow strip is infinitely easier to manage than the last one.

My back pressed against the wall, I sneak a look through

the small glass inserts in the door. I don't see much, but I do hear the voice of an Uuzik on the other side. I crouch down, making sure I'm hidden, but this means that I can't see him, either.

However, if the door happens to spring open for whatever reason, perhaps I can avoid his gaze long enough to rush the monster.

Too bad, though — that plan would go south quick. See, for my plan to work, that would be assuming that the Uuziks weren't prepared. But they evidently are, because as I ready myself to rush through the door for a quick strike, I get inside and am immediately tackled hard to the ground. I land with a thud, and my neck and head hang over the edge of the elevator shaft just far enough that one trip up would take my head clean off.

Gazing at my attacker, I see the disgusting hate-filled, grunting face of an Uuzik with his claws in the air ready to stab me. For a creature that's about my height with a rather scrawny frame, the Uuzik's full weight keeps me pinned down in his overpowering stance. He swings to my left first, so I bob and weave, trying to dodge each strike as his claws miss me. On his last strike, I manage to grab his wrist, avoiding his sharp claws and lifting myself up. I bench press his upper body as high as I can, and then with a swift kick, I send him tumbling to my left, removing him from me. We flip positions and I pin him down but, unlike his failure at killing me, I waste no time with my opportunity.

I restrain his claws again, and lift him up while I begin to stand. He makes a few clicking sounds to get out his last curse words, but I don't care what he has to say. I lift his arms above his head to expose his chest before kicking him into the elevator shaft. He falls straight down, careening like a rock into the black abyss below. I only hope the fall is as painful as he deserves.

Adrenaline pumping through my veins, I spin around, ready for round two, but the room remains empty. Probably for the best.

When the excitement dies down, I allow the joy of making it up one more floor to overtake me. Maybe it's not the end destination, but I'm finally going in the right direction. An improvement, if nothing else.

This room looks a fair bit different than anywhere I've seen previously. Of course, it still has the same steel walls and a bunch of different tables, but plastered on the walls are a multitude of maps.

I recognize a few of them, some displaying a decent chunk of the west galaxy and some showing the south side. On each of the larger galaxy maps are black Xs crossing out some of the planets, and a few others are circled in red with foreign writing underneath. Although I struggle to read the text, I can recognize some of the planets marked in red. Mainly JE-11 and DM-32, which gets my brain thinking.

I've made it into some sort of planning or strategy conference room. I'm a little surprised they'd have it in the basement, but I guess they want it hidden from...well, from people like me.

Underneath the bigger maps of the galaxy are tiny but more detailed maps of worlds. These ones have many more markings and notes, like a children's colouring book. From what I can gather, the Uuziks have marked out the spots that have creatures with traits they deem desirable for their master plan.

Speaking of plans, scattered about on the tables are a huge number of papers, all with writing in the native Uuzik language.

For a destructive, power-hungry race, the Uuziks conduct strategy meetings in a lot of similar ways to the Federation. What that says about the two parties involved…I'll let you decide.

If I'm in the strategy room, then the possibility of finding some valuable information is likely abundant, so I start investigating.

Unfortunately, most of the information laying around is tough to understand, and the things I can make out are rather pointless.

Eventually, I finally come across a few areas of interest in a folder underneath a stack of loose papers. I toss the useless ones to the floor and open up the folder, flipping through the notes. They're a series of grainy, black and white images that couldn't have been taken with modern-day technology. Under the photos are a few more notes.

I pull a conspicuous picture from the group that depicts a small black egg. I flip through the subsequent photos, and the egg continues to grow until I reach the back of the stack, where I see a poorly drawn rendition of the egg. What's relevant here is the arrow that points from the egg to another picture of the egg hatching, with the number 300 overtop of the arrow.

So…300 days until the egg hatches? Is that what this means? But what is the egg all about? The combination of their creatures filled with a Calax Crystal injection?

Next is another arrow, angled toward a very poor representation of a monster. It looks like a spider, but it has four legs instead of eight. I've seen better drawings from a six-year-old, so it's hard to tell. More Uuzik symbols are written on the paper, but they look out of place compared to everything else.

I keep digging until I find something rather intriguing — and a bit frightening — on the later pages. These ones are clear, and my visor can provide a loose translation for me:

Translation
---------------------------- Project BB - Project Obliterator,
Day 276: Progress Report

**"We are finally starting to move past the infantile stage of the lifeform, and substantial progress is being made. Once we pass the 300-day mark and the egg has matured its full cycle, we will be able to move on to phase two. The obliterator continues to be growing at a rate in which even we could not have predicted. We are still studying which of the DNA strands could be causing such rapid growth, but it is too early to say. Thanks to the fur of the treklet and that of the leijor, the specimen should be able to survive any planet's temperature, regardless of environment. This will allow it to sustain the length of life needed to redevelop itself after its life cycle ends.**

**Due to the Calax Crystals' rich core in RG–87, letting the lifeform rest in incubation while deep in the planet absorbing Calax Crystal nutrients will increase all aspects of production. We have made progress in harvest-**

ing the above surface crystals for a new supply when this planet is dead.

We have noticed a massive uptick in the lifeforce being drained from the planet's core to the point that even life on the surface has begun to notice. Thanks to the Calax Crystals embedded in its core, and the steady flow of the gems' power into the lifeform's body, the growth rate that would have taken half a dozen years will only take an estimated 300 days.

Once the egg begins to hatch around the planet's core, it will only take a few short days until it gains the full scope of its power. By this time, RG-87 will have nearly been drained of all lifeforce, and then our project will take care of the rest. After the lifeform has been sufficiently fed by the planet and the planet can no longer sustain its natural cycle, the lifeform will revert back to its larval stage and cocoon itself in another egg as an act of hibernation."

------------------------------------------------------------------------

I put the paper down while my jaw drops. Pausing to let the info sink in, I pick up the paper again and give it a second read. The words clearly didn't sink in the first time, but after confirming, it really hits me.

The first sign of bad news was that the ferocious skeletal dragon I fought was nothing more than a failed attempt at this Project BB. Not the real thing, like I hoped. It was probably just a poor combination of species and ingested Calax Crystals, if I had to guess.

Either way, the real threat this whole time has been laying deep in the planet's depths, resting and feeding until its strength reaches levels that I can't even begin to imagine.

When I give it a little more thought, the logic seems accurate. When I arrived on RG–87, the planet did look rather dead. From the wilting trees to the disgusting lake beside my landing point, all of it looked less like an untouched and uncultivated planet letting nature work its cycle and more like the life was being drained from it. Now I know why. The planet itself, the lives of the animals and plants—and, dare I say, any intelligent creatures—were having their lives syphoned from them. All in a lust to feed the insatiable appetite of whatever monster lay in waiting near the planets inside.

But the biggest question, and the one that I'm most scared to find the answer to, is how many days does this monster have left in incubation?

Based on the state of the planet, I'd say not many, if any at all.

With my mind now on the time, I glance to the corner of my visor and check my oxygen levels. Two hours, that's all. Now I can feel the looming tension begin to weigh me down. Each breath of air I exhale is one step closer to death, my life being drained just like the life of the planet I'm stuck on.

If nothing else, at this point I've gathered more than enough sufficient data on the Uuziks' plans and on Project BB to have a comfortable understanding of how it will work.

They'll take the monster in egg form, which I assume is a relatively small object, and move that tiny yet powerful weapon from planet to planet. They'll bury into the cores to live and grow, all while draining the lives of those above it until all life and the planets themselves rot away. And with the increased development speed thanks to the Calax Crystals, they'll be able to possibly create more and more of these abominations, letting them all chip away at the universe as they so choose. Although, I doubt that the entire universe is their main target.

I do know which planet they'll likely target first, and it's the most populated and prominent planet under the Federation's rule. Dubas.

After all, the two remain in an ongoing war, one that most feel will never end.

Of course, if the Uuziks manage to get this monster off, they'll be ending that war with a bang.

I'll admit for a brief moment that I wonder if getting rid of the Federation might be more beneficial than not, but the Uuziks being the reason for it? Not so much. A world based solely on power and strength… think of it. Even as a mercenary who'd likely have an upper hand in such a tyrannical galaxy, I can't live to see such a creation. The amount of lives lost, lives of beings who have nothing to do with the Federation, would be astronomical.

As the only one who knows the dangers on the horizon, I'm going to stop them, even if I have no duty to do so.

I just need to get that Federation beacon to the surface, and the SFF will come in waves to shut this place down. Project BB will be disposed of.

I do a quick check of the remaining papers, but find nothing of substance. A few small updates on Project BB, but they're more or less the same. It feeds, it grows bigger, the planet gets weaker, rinse and repeat.

Satisfied with what I've learned, I turn my attention back to escaping.

I make my way back to the elevator and jam the button on the side wall. Just as before, nothing comes down and I need to find a way up. Luckily for me, this floor has a few more rooms and doorways, which means that maybe I could find some stairs.

I continue onward, moving from room to room. They're empty and provide nothing much to see, but eventually I come to a small, arched opening. I stare up and see a familiar sight, one I actually feel happy about—or at least as happy as one could be given the circumstances.

I see the familiar cylindrical base of the tower with all the bridges crossing back and forth above me, each one climbing higher and higher.

A small glint of light beams down and fills me with hope. I can see the surface and taste the air of the outside world, and I can't wait.

But to really seal the victory and stick it to the Uuziks, I open up my wrist compartment and pop out the distress beacon. I punch in my old code, and this time it begins to glow blue and vibrate in my hand. The light continues to fade in and out, but it never turns off, meaning that the signal is being emitted to the Federation. Now all I need to do is get out and hope they arrive quick enough to get me out of here. Easier said than done with the time I have left, but hope is hope. And I have a lot of it right now.

Now if I were simply to play the good Samaritan role in this story, one could argue that the biggest part of my mission has come to an end. Regardless of the outcome, I've sent a distress call to the Federation, one that they'll no doubt investigate. Even their incompetence can put two and two together upon arrival and see that the Uuziks are plotting something. If I don't make it out alive, at least the rest of the galaxy will still be saved.

But I'm a mercenary, not a good Samaritan, and I have zero interest in dying. Especially not if it means that the Federation can take all of the glory for my hard work. No way am I letting that happen.

My next move is to escape this base and get as far from the tower as I can before the Uuziks catch on.

I step into another side door and look around. My paranoia…no, my instincts are going off like crazy, simply based on the fact that nobody appears to be around. I've hopped between at least five rooms on this floor, and aside from the close call with the Uuzik who jumped me, I've yet to see a soul.

Thinking back, even when I looked up the spire, no Uuziks were in sight. Something is amiss. It has to be some sort of trap being set up for me. Do they know I'm alive? I wouldn't put it past that monster Fenrich. But if they're preparing for my resurgence, I have no other choice — I'll just have to spring the trap. Time is of the essence, and with each passing second, I continue to drain my life's clock.

I cross the hall into the next room, still not seeing anybody. This room reminds me of the warehouse entrance — the entrance of the room I'm trying to get to.

The room is filled with crates, but they're far smaller than the boxes in the warehouse. When I crack one open, I expect to find even more surplus of Calax Crystals, but instead I find bottles stacked to the brim.

They're so jammed that I can't even move the boxes. Curious, I crack open a couple of other boxes and see some tools that are familiar and rather common. Others are strange; I've never seen them before.

This must be the different supplies with which to experiment on each creature. The Uuziks probably took the liberty of gathering each planet's resources as well. They won't stop until every planet in the universe is nothing but a dusty rock floating in space.

I grab a bottle from the crate and give it a once-over. It's the size of a water bottle, but it has a roundish bottom filled with murky, greyish-purple liquid. I pop open the lid, and smoke starts to rise as a potent odor punches me in the face. I stumble backwards and nearly drop the bottle, but luckily, I keep a tight grip.

Is this the serum they've been turning those Calax Crystals into?

I can't believe how much of the stuff they have. It's enough to inject every lifeform on the planet five times over.

Unless they're overloading animals with bottle upon bottle. That's how you end up with a mutant skeleton dragon thing roaming around, I guess.

A thought occurs to me: There's a chance that none of these serums are going to the entrapped creatures anymore. A chance that they're all being shipped down below to the lifeform that currently sleeps deep underground, waiting to finish its incubation.

I shudder at such a horrific possibility, keeping in mind what a mere sliver of a Calax Crystal did to my now-melted gun, or that using a small chunk almost fried my suit beyond repair, not to mention the damage caused to the creatures.

Yet this lifeform deep below can seemingly digest them with ease. How that's even possible is beyond me, but I have to prepare for such a scenario.

Since there's no other info about Project BB and all that remains are copious amounts of dangerous chemicals, I prepare to find my next destination when I hear a strange hissing sound from one of the crates on the east side of the room.

I've heard that sound before. But I can't quite place it. It's not a sound that Uuziks make, that's for sure. It's too high pitched. I follow the sound over to a cracked crate and regard it with skepticism. Despite opening a number of the boxes in the room, I can't recall cracking this one open. The slit of the lifted lid has barely enough room for me to get my fingers under it, but no more.

I should leave the box alone. I really should, but my stubborn brain is curious.

I jam my fingers inside and crouch down, ready to slide the lid off. But before I can, my head snaps back like I was just punched. I stumble from the sheer shock of it, smacking a couple of chemical boxes as I waver. I'm lucky the whole tower doesn't go up in smoke.

The crashing sound of the bottles hitting the ground would certainly be hard for anyone to ignore, as different substances spill and splatter all over the place. If the Uuziks didn't know I'm still alive before, this has most certainly clued them in.

I shut my eyes briefly in denial, but when I open them again, all I see is black. Only it's not black ink, or even a black streak. Whatever sits on my mask, it has certain texture to it. Fur. Fur that rubs back and forth while the owner of it hisses a violent whisper into my ears.

I reach up and grab whatever the hell is on my face with a death grip. When I feel its soft and fluffy body, I know my suspicions are right.

Try as I do, this thing refuses to let go as I pull hard enough to tear it apart. Sounds of metal crunching drown out the hissing, and I can feel the back of my head being squeezed tightly. This thing is squishing my helmet, hoping for my head to explode like a watermelon. I continue to yank and pull, but the creature refuses to concede. Finally, I give it a solid punch to the top of its head, and watch as two yellow glowing orbs appear on my visor like two distant planets in space. They have small slits of black in them, and they're definitely not planets. They're a pair of menacing eyes staring back at me.

Panicked, I grip the thing tighter, and it lets out a wincing cry. I manage to rip the creature off my visor, and without a second thought, I chuck the vermin into a crate on my left.

I catch my breath, and now I can see what got the jump on me, although after seeing those eyes just moments before, I had a pretty good idea.

"How the hell is this thing still alive?" I growl, ready to fight. "You're even more stubborn than I am."

The tiny beast pokes its head out before hissing at me again.

That treklet from the terrarium has made his way down to the basement first floor just to greet me. And it remembers me as well.

This isn't overly surprising, considering the way it cunningly and fiercely ripped through the Uuziks before. The thing is a killing machine, but to get down to the basement before Fenrich's men finally killed it is an impressive feat. After all, I would know.

It glares at me as I loom over it, looking as pleased to see me as I am to see it.

Instincts take over, and I reach for my gun. I'm ready to put an end to this bastard, but as I grasp at my holster it dawns on me: I have no blaster. And now comes a new problem.

The treklet begins leaping across container lids, bearing its sharp blood thirsty fangs that it desperately wants to sink into me.

I have to admit that even in a full suit of armor and cloaked in some of the strongest metals in the galaxy, going up against this twelve-inch furry woodland creature injects more fear into my veins than if I were fighting any Uuzik.

Before I can look for something to fight with, the treklet latches onto my left leg, sinking those potentially lethal fangs into my suit like a hot knife through butter. To say that they're as sharp as knives wouldn't do them justice. The treklet rips though my suit with ease, puncturing my leg. Luckily, it misses anything vital, but I still bite my lip in agonizing pain while trying not to make a sound. Still attached to me, I drop my fist on its head before grabbing its tail.

As soon as I clutch it, I feel the teeth sink further into my flesh, this time with even more anger in its bite. Suffice to say that treklets really, really don't like having their tails grabbed.

No matter how hard I try, I can't get this demon spawn off of me.

By nature, treklets are not a poisonous animal, and a bite will do nothing more than leave some scarring. But for all I know, this mutated monster has gained some poisonous ability thanks to these ridiculous experiments.

Tired of playing games, I decide to make use of what's in the room.

I grab whatever chemicals I can find and start lobbing them like grenades. They splash at and cover the creature while I'm still clutching its tail with one hand.

The pressure finally releases from my leg. I rip the treklet off, flinging it across the room.

It crashes into the wall, falling with a thud, but that isn't the end of this plight. I grab a glass bottle and chuck it toward the rabid-like freak. Purple liquid rains down on it, ruining the treklets coat of fur with messy, patchy stains.

The treklet lets out another angry hiss, and I know exactly what it's saying: "I'm going to kill you for that."

"The feeling's mutual," I want to retort, but instead I let my actions do the speaking for me. This ridiculous feud has run its course, and I'm done with it. Before it can pounce at me again, I reach for another tube, this one yellow, and whip it like a baseball.

The bottle smashes into the treklets face, glass penetrating its body. It screeches loud enough to alert everyone in the galaxy, but not because of the glass and the dripping blood. It cries out in agony because of the mixture of chemicals splashed onto its body. By perfect chance, the two liquids are highly reactive.

I brace myself for the unexpected as the chemicals take over my part of the fight.

Smoke from the treklet's fur rises to the ceiling as it

screams in agony. It begins to squirm back and forth on the ground chaotically, doing anything it can to release itself from the pain. It fights and begs for help to the point of almost making me regret my actions. Almost.

It fights for as long as it can, twisting and contorting desperately, but no amount of struggle helps. After what feels like an endless amount of time, the treklet finally ceases its fight, the violent light in its cat-like eyes fading into nothingness.

Being a mercenary can put one into a lot of tough and uncomfortable spots. I've seen many creatures die at the hands of other bigger monsters, and also, of course, by my own hand, but for some reason, this one hits different. Perhaps it's because of how much it's helped me, even if inadvertently. Or maybe it's because treklets are supposed to be a peaceful, non-hunting species and should have no business with me.

When I kill other beasts, it's because they're pre-disposed to kill me. This makes it an act of survival, but this poor treklet was never given the choice to fight. It had been chosen from its family and held for experimentation. No—that's being generous to the Uuziks. It was taken against its will and forced to pay with its life.

At least its pain is over. The treklet is clearly dead.

I pick him up and look at his ravaged body. I don't know why I do what I do sometimes, but I pop the lid off the crate from where he surprised me, and I lay him to rest. I close the makeshift coffin and give him a salute for all his help.

I'd have done more, but I'm still on borrowed time. I need to get moving.

With nothing left to do but head upward, I pull out my map and prepare to charter my course. Zooming in on a small tunnel route no bigger than a crawl space, it looks like it'll lead me directly to the first floor. I'm not sure if it's a vent or some Uuzik-made escape path, but it'll be more than enough for me to work with.

Once I sneak through to the first floor, all that will remain is to get through the warehouse garage I first entered from. After that, it's about getting as far away from this place as I can. I'll go literally anywhere else. And if I play my cards right, the Uuziks will never suspect a thing.

However, before any of that happens, I still need a bit of help. Luckily, I'm in just the room for a helping hand. I store as many chemical bottles as I can, safely in my suit. I keep them away from the remaining Calax Crystals, for obvious reasons.

Though I don't have traditional weapons on my side, I've witnessed firsthand the destructive power of these liquids when combined. With them, I might be able to escape an Uuzik or two if need be.

Obviously, the more ideal scenario would be not getting spotted at all, but after the day I've had, that feels like too much to ask. It also bears mentioning that I just put an end to the only other thing on this planet that was helping me dispose of the Uuziks.

And, of course, I can't forget the other risk I'm assuming in all this: If any of the vials break inside of my suit, I'm in a world of trouble. The last thing I want is to end up like that treklet I just laid to rest.

I take one more look at my oxygen clock. My time is precious. I have one hour left, and at this point, the only way I'll survive is if a Federation solider happens to be carrying spare oxygen tanks when I meet them. That seems unlikely, but with limited options, unlikely scenarios are all I have.

Walking out the door and further down the hall, I see some of the ceiling walls collapsed in, cutting off any regular route.

Something about this looks strange, though. The way the metal bars and debris fell in such a perfect blockade suggests that this is manmade. Or, more accurately, Uuz-ik-made. Are they scared of me, opting to block me in, instead of attempting to kill me? That would make sense, actually; I've survived far more mayhem than any of those bastards ever would.

I always found that one of the stranger parts to being a mercenary is how many times I end up in a tight crawl space on each mission. I'm not claustrophobic, believe me — if I were, I'd never have stepped foot in the Dynex suit, but that doesn't mean I am a fan of small spaces. Especially not in a broken-down metal suit filled to the brim with dangerous and highly reactive chemicals.

As it turns out, the small tunnel I found on the map is right next to the blockade. It's a side vent, but unlike the previous vents I traversed through before, these are nothing short of military training crawls. My arms are pinned to my side and my legs are clawing at the metal as I try to avoid making too much commotion. I'm stuck and committed to moving forward until I reach my destination. Then I'll have to pray that I can get out.

Everything around me is boxed into four metal walls. As silly as it sounds and despite my non-claustrophobic tendencies, my biggest fear has always been finding someone else and meeting them face to face in one of these places. If I found an Uuzik here, it's not like either of us would be able to free ourselves and attack, so nothing would likely happen anyway. But it's one of those weird fears, I guess.

Thankfully, that doesn't happen this time, and I'm able to crawl my way around and up a steep slope to the first floor.

After another 15 minutes of non-stop crawling, albeit inch by painfully slow inch, I reach the exit. But there, a new problem awaits me, the same one I seem to encounter often with these pesky crawl space vents.

The vent in the wall has metal bars that I can see through just fine, but what I can see is the far wall made of steel, and no floor. I try to inch closer without giving away my position until I can finally see my landing spot. Of course, it's a good eight feet below me. My only saving grace is that the vent leads me out into the stairwell between the first and second floor. If I time it right, nobody will see me.

Now comes the tricky part—getting out. See, if you think about it, the only way in is headfirst, and since I have no room to move, the only way out is…you guessed it: headfirst. Getting my legs out in front of me to stick the landing is impossible.

I groan silently, as I know what my only option is. I'll just have to suck it up and hope to cushion the fall with my arms. After twenty-two plus hours of this arduous, tortuous, grueling day, falling face first out of a hole in the wall is the last thing I want to be doing.

I suck in a deep breath and start to crawl again, gripping the ledge and pulling myself forward. I close my eyes and exhale. Calm and ready, I shoot myself forward with a combination of my thrusters and whatever strength I have left in my arms.

Crash, bang, boom.

I land on my forearms and my face with an incredible thud, and my legs fall over top of me, straightening me out so that I'm lying on my back. Unfortunately, that's about as smooth as it could have been to keep any vials — or vitals, like my organs — from breaking.

Rough landing behind me, on the other side of the door is the main bridge leading me to my freedom. I gingerly get to my feet and walk up to the small glass insert. I peek through just in time to see that the task in front of me won't be an easy one.

Ten, maybe twelve Uuziks are patrolling the bridge, walking back and forth with guns at the ready. They occasionally stop and talk to each other in their disgusting dialect before marching again.

Four are on the bridge while the remaining are all in front of the door to the warehouse entrance.

Looks like they don't want anybody getting in…or getting out.

Just 56 minutes of oxygen remains. Any which way I slice it, I'll be cutting things close.

Since I lack real weapons, fighting through the masses is going to be impossible. I need a new idea.

I thought that some chemical warfare would be helpful against one or two Uuziks, but this is too many to take out at once.

Now's a good time to shift my focus from taking out the

Uuziks for an escape, and instead toward creating a diversion.

Luckily for me, I have just the chemicals to pull off such a tactic. But the Uuziks are nowhere near close enough to my side of the bridge for me to act.

As much as I have no interest in drawing attention to myself, blowing my cover is the only way this will work.

I pull out a round bottle of the yellow liquid and pop off the lid, dump some purple liquid into it, and then watch as the glass starts to fume.

I spring through the door and lob the chemical bomb like a grenade into the center of the bridge. From there, the exploding glass will do a good amount of the work for me.

Yellow liquid sprays out, painting the bridge in rain drops as the purple instantly mixes in.

At the first indication of noise, every Uuzik turns in my direction, guns locked and loaded. It'll take them at least a second or two to realize where it's coming from, and that'll be all the time I need. I dive behind a stubby wall, getting on my hands and knees before starting to crawl. I lob another chemical into the pile, and this one creates far more chaos than the last two. I don't even care if I'm seen this time because I know what'll happen next...and it'll blow my cover regardless.

Boom.

Once all the chemicals mix, a massive explosion bursts out, sending Uuziks flying in all directions. Smoke, debris, Uuzik body parts—everything goes flying, including the bridge's center half. That, I certainly am not prepared for. It's starting to crumble. I might have just screwed myself.

Through the smoke, I scramble to my feet and take off

in a kamikaze dash. I have no idea if this is the right move or not.

With my visor, I can see clearly enough through the smoke to maneuver my way past all obstacles, including the massive gap in the bridge I created.

Both sides of the bridges are beginning to collapse, and I can feel my feet stumbling along the way. At any point, the next step I take might be my last.

The pain in my legs keeps shooting through my body, courtesy of the treklet bite marks. But the pumping adrenaline acts as a decent cure.

Dashing through the fire (that I partly caused), I hit the end of my road and leap toward the other end of the bridge. I activate my thrusters to help me across, this causes even more flames to burst out through the smoke.

When landing, I roll and find myself next to a panicked Uuzik. Before he can react, I wrestle him over the edge of the bridge in an act of vengeance.

I can see the claws of other Uuziks hanging off the bridge, one slip away from death, but my head stays down and I keep running. My only hope is that the Uuziks blocking the front entrance are compelled to help their brethren rather than chase me, but of course I underestimate the Uuziks' lack of compassion. Power is all that matters to this race, and they only see Uuziks begging for help as a weakness.

The second they catch a glimpse of me through the smoke and mayhem, they turn heel and begin to chase. Sizzling sounds of plasma bullets zoom past my head, hitting the crates of the warehouse. I haul myself to the finish line. I can see it in sight.

More blasts whip past me as the Uuziks rush through the door, their aim nowhere near as good as mine.

I practically glide along the ground in a 100-meter sprint that would set records. I feel a slight sting in my right shoulder but keep running. I guess not all Uuziks have bad aim. But one hit won't stop me.

That said, the warehouse doors coming to a close just might.

Smack in front of me and where the gleaming light of my freedom stands, two steel doors are gradually converging, ready to lock me in. Someone must have hit an emergency alarm again or something, because the red lights start flashing like when I reached the top floor. A second sting shoots up my left leg with a deep burn. Another plasma blast lands. The shots are slowing down, but they're getting more accurate.

I'm only a few feet away and I keep storming forward. I make a diving roll as the doors slam shut.

# *PART 4*
## *AN UNLIKELY TEAM*

I HAVEN'T SEEN SUNLIGHT IN AGES. NO—I GUESS that's not entirely true, but that's what if feels like after spending so much time in the dank and dire Uuzik base.

And now, as I dive through the steel doors to escape this prison, I'm so grateful for the beaming rays of sun that blind me momentarily. I'm free. I'm finally free, and, better yet, I still have about 45 minutes of oxygen to spare. I never thought I'd be so happy to see the decrepit wastelands and rotting grass of RG–87. But here I am, absolutely in love with the sight of it.

But actually, the planet looks even worse than when I arrived almost 24 hours prior. The sky remains blue, but it has streaks of grey clouds beginning to form en masse. The dirt ground is even more brittle and dried up, to the point that I'm amazed my barrel roll stunt didn't shatter the ground beneath me.

Time is running out—not just for me, but also for the planet. Clearly, it won't be long until Project BB finishes feasting and leaves nothing but a dust ball in its wake.

Hopefully, the Federation will arrive in time to bring a halt to the ever-growing lifeform, but my hopes of them being around the corner have been spoiled. I see no ships flying overhead, no soldiers on the ground, and no help on the horizon.

Even though I won the battle by successfully escaping, I might lose the war thanks to the Feds' lack of response.

What I do hear, however, is the screeching metal doors once again. But this time, they're opening back up. Just because I escaped the base doesn't mean I'm in the clear, not by any stretch. These Uuziks are beginning to hate me as much as I hate them, and they aren't about to remain bound to their base. As long as I'm running, they'll be chasing.

Without looking back, I sprint to my left while a few plasma blasts soar over me. Now the Uuziks are just blindly firing while the door opens.

I use the door as cover, following behind as it opens up. I glance around feverishly. There has to be somewhere to go. Anywhere?

The doors fall back into place, sounding like heavy anvils coming to a stop. My shield is gone, and now I'm at the edge of the base's side. I turn left and find three speeder bikes sitting idle, ripe for the taking. They're no different than the one I stole and rode to the base early this morning. At least this time, I know how to make them work.

I don't care if there are Uuziks nearby or if this is some sort of ambush. I hop on the closest bike and take off, tearing down the dirt path as fast as this thing could go.

Hitting open land, I glance back and see two Uuziks mounting the other bikes. These guys are persistent, I'll give them that.

To make things worse, I have no destination in mind for my escape. From what I know of the planet, searching for help is a no go. Finding a village or civilization not already wiped out by the Uuziks also seems unlikely.

It doesn't take long for plasma pistol shots to begin hurling past me. I try to look back amid the high-speed chase, and I can loosely make out four Uuziks. There are only two bikes hunting me, but each one has an Uuzik driver and an Uuzik gunner. As a solo rider, I clearly have no way of fighting back, so I continue to push the threshold of my speeder's limits.

I swerve as best I can, trying to avoid giving them a steady shot, but with each move off of true north, the gap between us closes. They follow me like my own shadow, and since we're on empty terrain, I'm a sitting duck.

The chase keeps up for a few precarious minutes. Everywhere I turn and with every maneuver I pull, the Uuziks stay right on my tail. It's desperation time. I stare ahead, feeling the rush of air forcing me back into my seat. Then I look down at the dashboard controls and see that my gas is running on empty.

*Oh, come on!* I silently yell. I've definitely had enough. I grip the throttle in one hand and call up my map with the other. It projects in front of me, and because of my speed it struggles to keep a steady picture. But there's no way I'm slowing down. It would be the death of me.

Driving and looking at a static map is no easy task and highly not recommended, but in such open space, I have nothing in front of me to fear…or at least that's what I thought. As it turns out, there's a cliff only a few kilometers away, and it's as wide as it is large.

From the way my map projects it, the chasm looks like a giant rift in the planet, and it goes farther than my map can display.

Seeing no other option, another crazy and downright reckless idea springs into my head: My only hope is to leap the chasm. Yes, it's dangerous, and I can't guarantee I have the remaining fuel to pull off such a dumb feat, but it's not like I have a bunch of options. Besides, if there's one thing I can guarantee, it's my death if those Uuziks get me.

I take another check of my oxygen. Only 30 minutes left. My time is up—I'll just have to come to grips with it. The Federation isn't showing up to save me.

Steadying myself, I grip the handlebars and throttle the bike. Then I crouch down, making myself—hopefully—as aerodynamic as possible.

In just moments, I feel the steadiness of a smooth ride go out from under me and, before I realize it, I'm soaring through the air like a dorneal.

For a second, this weightless feeling makes me want to vomit. And I know that if I look down, that feeling will only increase. But when I feel gravity start to kick in and my body descend, I know it's about to be trouble.

The bike is dipping faster than expected, and at any moment I'll be plummeting to my death. I'm only at about the halfway point of the chasm. At this rate, I'll be lucky to just crash into the cliff wall.

Although, the good thing is that I've actually anticipated such a failure. In fact, the plan had never been to make the jump with my bike intact, but only to use it as a leaping point.

Before I begin my dramatic decent into death's clutches, I stand up on the bike, working hard to maintain my balance. I hold firm, standing high on the seat like a circus performer, all while dipping downward. I can feel the burn in my legs as I muster their remaining strength.

Another few seconds pass, and the same internal pressure that weighed me down as I fell through the spire returns. I take a deep breath and regain my composure. One final step to go. At this point, I've forgotten all about the Uuziks even chasing me. They play no part in the equation anymore.

I ride the bike as far as it'll take me, and now it's time to say goodbye. I springboard off, feeling daggers stab through my brittle legs. The bike shoots down below me, dropping like a stone into the chasm, never to be seen again.

Soaring through the air, I know I'm closer but still falling short. I need more height for my plan to work. Once again, I call on my thrusters to provide aid.

I've said it before and I'll say it again: The Dynex suit may be the greatest invention of all time. Even if the Bacardi sent me on this mission in the first place, the amount of good will they've built up in terms of this suit far exceeds the countless close calls with death this trip has caused.

It's like my suit had been made with fingernails in mind; I easily grab the ledge of the cliff with them. My legs and body smack against the rock wall, but I tighten my grip and hold on for dear life. As worried as I am about the lack of strength in my arms, my biggest concern is the frail state of the planet itself. The tightness of my grip could possibly crumble the dirt and drop me to my death.

I look down. This is a dumb idea. I close my eyes, feeling the strain on my muscles and my weightless, dangling legs. I don't know how I manage to pull myself up, but since I've survived up to this point, giving up seems like a stupid idea.

On the bright side, as I dangle above my almost-certain pit of death, I hear four consecutive cries that disappear into the abyss, along with what sounds like two explosions. There's no doubt that the Uuziks hot on my tail were dumb enough to attempt such a misguided leap of faith.

Well, either that or they were about to return to their tyrant leader Fenrich emptyhanded, which would no doubt lead to an even less-merciful death. These Uuziks are in the same no-win situation as me.

I grip the ledge, praying for it to hold strong, and then I pull myself up. When I toss my legs over, I roll onto my back and try to catch my breath.

A few tense inhales and exhales later, I sit up, looking across the chasm in front of me. Nothing but vast, empty space. I turn around, and behind me is even more wasteland. Nobody is around. No Uuziks. No creatures. Just desolate land and darkening skies.

I must've traveled far enough to where the Uuzik base has faded entirely from sight, since I can't see it any longer.

The corner of my visor flashes with 15 minutes of oxygen left, and I let out a deep sigh. Now I'm really out of time. The counter has never gone this low on me before, and although I'm confident that the time is accurate, I don't really know to what degree. Do I really have 15 minutes left in my life? Is there a chance it could be a slight bit more? Or worse…less?

I pull out the distress beacon and watch as it flashes, not that it matters now. Like the grains of sand in a doomed hourglass, the time for rescue has run out. Each flash, in precise intervals, mocks my hopes. The Federation will let me down once again. No big surprise, I guess. But no matter. When they finally find my body, I'll be out of air. Dead.

It's strange, the thought of waiting patiently for your death. Not waiting for someone to kill you, but just sitting down with nobody around, and knowing that at any moment, your life will be taken from you.

I drop my shoulders and toss the beacon of hope backwards, and it bounces a few meters away. I have no use for the piece of junk anymore.

Deciding to get comfortable in my final moments, I return to lying on my back. The sky is far from a pretty sight to stare at, but I'm fairly blind to it at this point anyway. I don't care.

Thoughts of what the future might hold rush to my mind. Not necessarily what the future might hold, but what dying hold. Some races in the universe believe in a higher power, and that when you die, you go to the sanctuary created by that power. Others believe that your soul will be placed into someone else, maybe a newborn baby. As for me, I haven't thought about any such beliefs. If there's some sort of afterlife, I'll be able to see my parents again at least, but even that doesn't add much consolation. I was so young when they died, so it's not like I had much of a relationship with them or many memories to relive.

But I decide that there's no use in thinking about "what-ifs." Whatever happens will happen, whatever will be will be, and embracing acceptance is all I can do.

My eyes begin to flutter closed as I try to drift asleep. After all, it'll be much less painful to die in my sleep rather than being conscious of it.

Suffocation is a fate I'd always hoped to avoid. As a mercenary, everyone knows the possibility of death is around any and every corner. My entire livelihood is predicated on taking dangerous missions, and then undertaking them with a high degree of success. All while putting myself in harm's way that, again, no sane person would ever do.

Frankly, none of that ever made a difference to me. I have no family to go back to, nor do I ever stay in a place for more than a few days at a time, which means I never have any time or ability to build relationships. Probably only a few Bacardi will notice because they'll lose their most trusted worker. But they'll be even angrier about not getting their Calax Crystals.

The dire countdown of my oxygen keeps ticking away, and a part of me wants to look. As one could expect, when you know ahead of time that your death is only minutes away, being able to relax and fall asleep is not particularly easy. Also, I technically failed my mission, so there's no sleeping easy with that one.

But I've done enough heavy lifting. If nothing else, I can take solace in the fact that the Federation will eventually arrive and hopefully put a stop to the Uuziks' plan. If they manage to complete that mission, then my failure won't be entirely in vain.

As much as I hate to admit it, this task is best left to a massive raid with a large-scale army, not one solo mercenary.

My eyes feel heavy, and each thought becomes fuzzier than the last. The toll of my final 24 hours is catching up to me. I figure I only have about five minutes left. Maybe.

I wonder if the Federation will hold a funeral for me. Though they'd have to find my body first, and that's highly unlikely.

Finally, I chuckle to myself thinking, I'm minutes away from dying and these are the thoughts I have before I go. Wondering about a funeral from a group of elites that I hate. I'd always expected something more philosophical for my last thoughts. I'll admit that I'm disappointed in myself for not being more astute or clever.

I can't believe how long this is taking. It has to have been 15 minutes by now. It feels like I've been sitting and reflecting for at least an hour. Did my timer malfunction when I restarted my suit?

I can't resist anymore. I open my eyes and sneak a glance at it. Three minutes left. Sigh.

Perhaps I'm right and my timer is off. Or maybe I just need some patience, not that it will change anything. Even if I try to get up, my body will refuse every command. All tanks of energy and all adrenaline reserves are emptied the second I hit the ground.

I crank my neck to look at the wrist compartment on my left arm. I thought-provoke the compartment to slide open, and it reveals one remaining Calax Crystal. It has a dull glow to it. Although those crystals helped me in a few pinches, unless they can produce oxygen, this last crystal will do absolutely nothing for me. Hard to believe that all this started over such tiny little crystals, and even more difficult to believe that they'd end up causing my death. I close my eyes and drift off again.

I don't want to watch the final minute of my timer count down. I'd rather let everything fade to black.

10 seconds. 9…8…7…6…5…4…3…2…1…


The afterlife has streaks of blurry, florescent yellow lights that mimic a water painting. Mixed in with those are plenty of grays that resemble the background of a steel roof. Not quite how I pictured my eternal bliss.

Or did I just wake up from my nap and am staring at the sky? If that's the case, RG-87's sky has changed drastically in my short slumber.

My eyes flutter open. I force out a yawn and try to adjust my body.

While the portrait returns to focus, I realize that what I thought was a sky is actually no such thing. It's a metal roof above me, with a bunch of rectangular tiles.

Okay, now I'm confused. My chest is rising and falling, but, more importantly, I can feel oxygen circulating though my nostrils. The air smells like the old Federation hospitals. I'd never forget that pungent stench.

Breathing seems unnecessary if I am, in fact, dead. On the other hand, I'm not looking through my visor, which explains the bright light blinding me. I have no vision dimmer, which I'm so accustomed to.

I lift my hand, blocking the light mercilessly beaming down on me. My arm is bare. Not taking my suit with me to the grave makes sense, but I'll admit, not having it isn't my ideal. There's valour and glory in that thing.

I try to sit up, but my body refuses. My arms are free, but my legs, head, and neck are stagnant. I take my other free arm and touch my forehead, feeling a thick leather strap that seems to be there as a headband. The sensation jogs my senses, and I notice a strange pinch on my nose and mouth. I slide my fingers down and grab a plastic mask that's stuck to my face. Although it's thin enough, I'm compelled to peel it off.

Now I have serious questions. I'm alive, which is good news. At least, I have to assume that I'm alive, because this would be far too weird of an afterlife.

There are few things, if any, that I can say that I know with confidence about the afterlife. But in heaven, hell, and everywhere in between, I firmly believe that you won't end up with a leather strap around your head after death.

This train of thought leaves me with two paths to go down. The first is that perhaps a drifter found me and managed to keep me alive long enough to get me to safety. It's a long shot. And the second thought is, why would anyone have strapped me to a dentist chair by my forehead?

But there's another scenario, one that's far scarier: The Uuziks somehow found me, and they're not interested in letting me die easy, instead taking me back to their base to torture me into giving them information about my suit. If the latter proves true, rest assured that I'll be dead in short order.

A few small beeps sound from my left, and then I hear a door opening from the same direction. Of course, I can't turn my head to actually see this visitor, but I'd be lying if I said that my initial thoughts weren't something along the lines of, *Well if I wasn't dead before, I'm definitely about to get killed now...*

A voice speaks, and the words are in plain English. He's not talking directly to me, so I assume he's here with colleagues. Making out the words is hard because of the beeps and groans of surrounding machines, so all that I manage to pick up is a very matter-of-fact voice saying, "Remove the mask."

Upon hearing those orders, I instinctively try to object, but when I open my mouth, nothing comes out. I don't know if the mask is keeping me from speaking or if my mind still hasn't recovered enough to formulate sentences, but, either way, I have no say in their decision.

Before long, I see a man cautiously standing over me, blocking out most of the light. His hair is brown and comes down past his ears, and a pair of large, round glasses indicates that he's some sort of scientist. A second scientist enters into and then walks out of my view, and then I hear a click, followed by a release of pressure on my forehead.

I hear a second click, and then the mask around my face lifts. I take my first breath of non-filtered oxygen in about 24 hours, and it feels incredibly amazing. My chest expands twofold as I inhale deeply and then gradually let it all out. I've missed effortless breaths.

My fascination with my ability to breath (it's amazing the things we take for granted) is soon interrupted by a human touch on my arm. There's another sensation I rarely feel since I wear my suit so often.

Free to move, I crank my neck to the left so that I can see who's given me the privilege of breathing again.

I'm wrong on one front, though. The second man in the room turns out not to be a scientist, or even a doctor. His silver and gold uniform and the spaceship emblem on his chest tell me all I need to know. But when the man speaks, I have no doubt who he is.

"Can you sit up, solider?" he says in a poised yet affirmative tone, one I unfortunately recognize all too well.

However, I release my brief disdain and attempt to answer his question. Besides, I'm curious if my body will allow me to sit up.

I reach for the edges of the narrow bed and push myself up and into a more comfortable position. Since I'm flat on my back, I need to move my entire body, something that turns out to be far more difficult than expected. I make a grunting noise and eventually manage to turn my body and toss my legs over the side.

Once I'm sitting and stable, I can confirm two things. First, the room I'm sitting in. It's a scientific examination area where people are monitored for health and recovery after traumatic events. Second, the identity of the man who's giving me these orders.

The man stands tall and has perfect posture, his arms behind his back. He wears a silver hat with gold trimming, a uniform only Sergeants in the Federation earn.

In the Federation, there are six rankings. Starting from the top: Commander, Sergeant, Lieutenant, Colonel, Private, Trainee. Within those are a few more different classes for each rank, and each class of the Federation is apparent from a simple glance of their uniform.

Commander, being at the top of the chain, never participates in any active missions, at least not from what I've seen. They're known more for living their cozy lives back on Dubas, making rules and regulations for the Federation. Basically, this means that when it comes to the Federation's day-to-day tasks and running a crew, the Sergeants are head of the pack. Among the group of Sergeants though, one of them reigns supreme above all else as the Commander and Chief. He makes all the final decisions on Federation fleets, and controls most if not all strategies on every large-scale situation, along with having his own individual fleet to control. Almost everyone in the universe would consider this role to be the most powerful one in the galaxy. And this very man happens to be standing right in front of me.

Sergeant Rupert Falcon Scott. He's revered by everyone in both the Federation and in most of the known universe. He has countless heroics under his belt, an unwavering pulse that can calm the masses, and is the leader this Galaxy needs.

But I think what makes people all over space revere him—especially the more common citizens of Dubas and beyond—is how many chances he's had to move up in rank to Commander. He could have taken the easy path and lived out most of his days with a fat, guaranteed paycheck, making minimal and trivial decisions about the universe without a second though. But he continually refuses the prospect of an easy life, and instead opts to remain living his days floating through space on a city-sized ship. Certainly, sitting on Dubas would provide less life and death moments for him, too. Perhaps he could even settle down and have a real family.

But that's not what he wants. Because as far as the Sergeant is concerned, he has a family: every single being within his crew and on their ships. He holds his crew as his highest priority, never letting any of them succumb to danger with a "no man left behind" mentality. You wouldn't always know it by the way he treats people, but it's obvious to me. I've got him all figured out.

That being said, I also know him as something entirely different: the pain in my ass. Even so, I still try to show a moderate amount of respect for the man, since despite him being such a frustration, it's fair to assume that his crew just saved my ass from the grips of death. Without his crew, I'd be decaying on RG-87, just like the planet itself.

With so many thoughts racing through my mind, I remain silent and let the Sergeant speak again.

"It's been a long time…Rimor." He pauses before he says my name — for dramatic effect, I suppose. He drops his salute and reaches to feel my forehead. If anyone else in space had reached to put their hand on me, I would've smacked it away, refusing to be treated as some kind of sickly infant, but for the Sergeant, I refrain. And there's a specific reason for that.

Although he's, without a doubt, a huge thorn in my side, he's also the closest thing to family that I have in this universe.

With the back of his hand, he presses my forehead and I finally answer his greeting. "It's only been…what — three years, maybe four?" I smirk slightly, then gently grab his hand by the wrist and push it away from me. Part of me wants to see how coordinated I still am, since my body feels otherworldly.

I look up at him and speak again. "So…care to explain what the hell happened? Or what I'm doing here?"

"Well," the Sergeant starts, adjusting his shoulders and clearing his throat. "We received a distress call from one of the Federation beacons. As I'm sure you're aware, this is not my crew's typical territory. But a few days ago, another fleet filed a missing person's report on one of these outer planets. My crew just happened to be passing by when the signal hit our computers, so we made a beeline to the call. Then when I touched down, lo and behold, I find our beacon sitting in a pile of dirt. I took a little look around, and probably two minutes later I stumbled across your rotting corpse on the ground. You're lucky I had spare oxygen tanks on me, or you would've suffocated. I don't know how long you went without air, but I have no doubt you were on the verge of death. I brought you back to the ship and strapped you to an oxygen tank to see if you would recover. You're lucky—our tests seem to show no significant brain damage from the lack of oxygen."

I must've passed out just before they arrived. I guess that beacon came in handy after all...

I look at the other scientists who helped save my life and then back at the Sergeant. "Well...um...thank you, I guess...for, you know—saving my life." The gratitude in my words is genuine, but interacting with the leader of the SFF doesn't come naturally to me as it does for most others. Plus, I hate having to thank him, no matter how grateful I am.

With the hope of avoiding any more awkward conversations, I attempt to stand up, but the Sergeant and the other scientist hold their hands out to stop me.

"Easy there," the Sergeant cautions me. "Try to take it slow for a few minutes. We pumped you full of oxygen, so you'll feel dizzy for a quite a while." The Sergeant brings his hands back to his side, but his eyes remain deadlocked with mine. "Give it a few minutes first, and when you feel you're ready, come and see me in my office. We still have more to discuss. That is, if you still remember where my office is." This time, it's the Sergeant's turn to offer a sly smirk.

I nodded silently. For some reason, when he talks to me in that concerning tone it always comes across as if he is talking down to me. I don't know if others hear it the same way or if it's my displeasure that makes his words sound the way they do. Either way, I let the comment slide.

Of course I know where his office is. When you spend the better part of your childhood in a little slice of hell like that, you don't just forget. At least this time I know that I won't be met with drills, strategy meetings, lectures, and Lord knows what else.

After the Sergeant leaves, I immediately stand up. Not that I care to admit it, but when I do stand up, I have to sit right back down; stars and spots are filling my vision. I take the few minutes granted to me to acclimate before attempting to rise again. Each step still has an out-of-body feel to it—walking, using my arms, and even moving my eyes come with difficulty. I decide to walk around the square room and take in my surroundings while I get comfortable.

I'm understandably curious about where I've been taken, although I do have a pretty good guess. The room is without question a medical center, with a half-bubble-shaped roof where metal bars and florescent lights are lined up across it. To my left is a long rectangular window, beyond which a few doctors are watching me like a zoo animal. More than likely, they're monitoring my progress and keeping me alive, so in a way I sort of owe them some gratitude, too. I count seven of them, which to me is a bit of overkill, but again—this is the Federation, so maybe not.

After giving myself about 15 minutes, I try again. Every movement is sluggish, like someone who just came out of surgery, but I begin to get my feet back under me after a few steps.

In many ways, it reminds me of the first time I stepped out of the Dynex suit after a long stretch. Often times, I can go days locked in that suit, not stepping out of it once, but when I finally do exit that other body, I walk like a newborn fawn. I think it has to do with the decreased weight on my frame, but I've never actually studied the effect.

With reasonable control over my body again, I take one final look at the rectangular window filled with scientists. They're talking amongst each other while still jotting down notes, monitoring my every move. They're just doing their jobs, so I don't know why seeing them bothers me so much. But it does. They're treating me as if I'm some sort of guinea pig in their lab, about to be experimented on.

Either way, I give them a mocking salute like the Sergeant did, and I head out the door. I'm half-expecting them to tell me that I need more time to get used to my newfound consciousness, but no such orders come. Not that it matters—I don't need their approval to leave. I'm not part of the Federation. They have no authority over me.

Once the door slides open, I see the long hall coated in metal rims, and every question about where I am is answered.

The most recognizable ship in the Federation's seemingly limitless fleet of ships is named Crimson Tide. I don't know who named it, but what I do know is that Crimson Tide is entrusted to only the highest of authorities.

Crimson Tide is comparable to a small city. And, in many ways, it has more benefits than some cities on Dubas does. Hospitals and medical treatments, lots of different places to eat, and beds for all the Federation soldiers. It also acts as a home for those who worked on the ship doing more remedial jobs — cooks, janitors, and even warehouse suppliers. All of them are considered integral parts of the ship.

This is the Sergeant's home, and a home for many others. On the Crimson Tide, you rarely step foot on other planets for more than a day at a time. When the mission is done, you return to the ship, ready to tackle the next call. In a way, we're similar in that style of living. Always on the move, never getting bogged down in one spot. I do it because that's how my job works, but I also like to see what the universe has to offer. With so many planets and species, a new adventure is always on the horizon. I don't know why the Sergeant does it, though.

Shortly after getting halfway through the rounded tunnel down the hall, the steel walls are replaced by long transparent windows looking out into space.

Since I'm not in any rush, I stop to admire the view. RG-87 floats miles over the horizon. It looks so small from where I'm standing, but I figure that due to the Uuziks' presence, the Feds want to keep a safe distance and not give away any surprises.

The rescue mission that saved me, I assume, had involved only a few small ships close to the size of my former ship, and they moved in so as to not cause any major disturbances. Obviously, the only other known race on RG-87 is the Uuziks, but the Federation has no way of knowing that, and they always follow protocol when it comes to their missions.

But even from such a distance, I can see that the planet is in dire straits. A massive black cloud has formed over the planet's visible half, looking like the eye of a hurricane. I swear that I can see sparks of lightning as well, but that might be a bit of a stretch. Every second, the planet grows worse, and in due time it'll cease to exist. All thanks to this Project BB.

Seeing the terminal state of the planet and armed with the knowledge of the Uuziks' plan, I can't help but wonder: What is the Federation waiting for? Do they just think someone with a distress beacon died on that planet for no good reason? Because they had nothing better to do? The Federation knows that the beacon doesn't belong to me.

Obviously, they need to investigate the issue. And soon.

In a lot of ways, this might be what bothers me the most about the Federation. They have more manpower than any force in the galaxy, weapons and artillery that would terrify anyone with a sane mind, and some of the best technology ever created in history. And yet when a planet stands on the verge of dying at the hands of a group of space terrorists, they do nothing. A group of space terrorists, I'd like to point out, that wants them dead more than anything else in the universe. But here we are, floating on a giant metal fortress in space, watching and waiting. Never acting. I know they have rules and protocols, and those are in place for a reason, but at some point, you need to act.

I walk past the glass inserts, and after taking another right, I find myself nearing the front of the ship. I head up a flight of stairs and take another right, ending up at the bow of the ship.

The bow is made of two different floors, with stairs in the middle connecting them. The upper deck hangs partially over the lower one, but it's only about half the size. There are ten people working away on different machines and computer systems, while on the lower deck there are closer to 50 people doing the same thing. And that's considered a light load. The other half must be on lunch or who knows where — it's the Federation, after all. I recognize almost none of these faces, but that's fine since I have no desire to be reacquainted with the ones I do know on this ship.

Each worker has a specific job on the Crimson Tide, and it almost never changes from day to day. Most of it has to do with weaponry and planetary research, but others have resource management and administrative positions. It takes a lot to keep a ship of such magnitude running at optimal efficiency.

I know that I'm at the front of the ship due to seeing the gigantic transparent windshield that looms over everyone.

Ignoring the strange looks I get as an unfamiliar face on the ship, I climb the next set of stairs up to the tiny third-floor balcony. That's my destination. As they say, the king sits atop the throne, and so too does the Sergeant sitting atop the Crimson Tide.

He's not the only one on the third floor, though. In fact, many of the beds for soldiers are located here.

The enclosed hallway is long and uninteresting. Plenty of doors and name plates, but that's about it. This part of the ship never seems to change.

At the end of the hall is my door, with a specific emblem on it to represent the Sergeant's quarters.

"How did I ever forget this place?" I groan, remembering hearing the Sergeant's words when he asked me to come up here.

I go to knock on the door, but anxiety rushes over me. There's no danger, I don't have to take orders from the Federation, and they can't do much to me. Still, an abundance of repressed memories are starting to creep back up. Not on my watch, though.

Instead of knocking, I barge in like I'm the Sergeant. Part of me does this to show my lack of respect for the Federation, and the other part of me can't just sit and wait to be granted entrance while all these mental spectres from the past continue to swarm me.

To my annoyance, but really not to my surprise, the Sergeant isn't even in his office. I roll my eyes; I should've known better than to think that he'd wait for me.

When I stroll in, the first thing to catch my eye is the number of picture frames hanging on the walls.

Some are of the Sergeant and a few children he's rescued, depicting the few times anyone can say he wears a genuine smile. Other photos show him with his reporting comrades. He comes off much stricter in those photos, but it's more of a front than anything else. That front does come naturally to him, though.

Although he considers the Crimson Tide soldiers and crew his family, he has no actual blood relations to speak of. His wife died many, many years ago, and his family mysteriously disappeared one day when he was growing up. Such events and the hurt and despair they caused often lead people to speculate that he lives on the Crimson Tide so religiously in order to escape it all.

I've never broached the topic before, and I'm not about to.

The one photo that takes me by surprise is sitting on the left wall by itself. The Sergeant and I are in full Federation uniform, and I'm giving a salute while he stands with his arms behind his back. Looking back at me in my younger years, I almost don't recognize myself. I look a fair bit older now, despite the picture only being taken seven years ago.

I'm 17 in the photograph. To graduate the preliminary Federation recruitment process, you're required to be a minimum of 18-years-old. I've never been overly patient, though. After some long negotiations with the powers that be, I was allowed to take the graduate test at 17. To everyone's enormous surprise, I passed with one of the highest grades in Federation history. Even more amazingly, I'm still not the youngest to ever do it, either. A few years before I was even born, a young girl managed to pass at the age of 16. I've never met her, but I know the hell I went through to graduate so early, so I can't fathom being a year younger and reaching those heights.

In the picture, neither of us are cracking a smile, but I knew then that he was pleased; he just wanted to avoid showing any bias.

I can't help but feel that the Sergeant having that picture on his wall is a rather arrogant move on his part. To pretend he was somehow my father figure, or even my family at all, feels disingenuous to say the least.

Aside from that, the room itself befits a Sergeant in every way. It's far larger than the other quarters on the ship, with copious shelving space filled with various books, maps, and other stuff that relates to the studies of different planets, along with a law book on Federation rules.

I must've read every book on this wall four or five times. They're all various strategy theory books, or rules and regulations from different governments in the universe.

When you're an intergalactic peacekeeper, it helps if you know all the rules that each planet abides by. I don't understand keeping the books myself, the space internet has all the information you could ever need. But, similar to his family life, it's none of my business.

On the far end of the room sits a desk as wide as I am tall, with a Federation banner strapped from one end to the other. He also has a handcrafted chair adorned with strange markings. It truly is an office fit for a man of his stature, despite how much I hate being in here.

A few moments pass, until I hear the door open behind me. In walks the Sergeant, exhibiting perfect posture.

"Thanks for coming," he greets me, sidestepping past me to get to his chair. He gestures for me to sit down on one of the plainer chairs in front of him. I do so, crossing my legs and making myself at home. I've sat in this exact chair hundreds of times before.

"So," he starts, looking less than pleased with what I've

been up to. "Are you gonna tell me what you were doing on a decaying planet on the edge of the galaxy?"

I pause, carefully thinking every word through before speaking. There's no way I'm telling him about my hunt for Calax Crystals; even though they're not for my benefit, the shady business deals would be called into question.

Keeping the conversation as vague as possible, I let the Commander and Chief of the Crimson Tide in on the Uuziks' plan.

"I was doing a little material collecting for the Bacardi from the Indigo when I ran into a small problem, as I'm sure you're aware."

The Sergeant raises one eyebrow. I can tell he's not buying it.

"It's unlike you to have trouble with just a simple material collection mission, so I'll take it that your lack of oxygen and the condition we found you in were partly due to the Uuziks that've been occupying RG-87 for the last year or so."

"Yeah, I…whoa, wait a second. You've known they've been occupying the place for a year?" I'm now raising my voice at him. "If you knew that already, why haven't you gone down and put a stop to them?!"

I resist the urge to stand up and slam my fists on the table.

"I can't believe you! You've been floating around here watching that planet die at the hands of the Uuziks for a year, and yet the best you've done is send a few ground troops down?!" I pause slightly and take a breath; I need to temper myself. "But of course that's what you did. I shouldn't even be surprised. That's all the Federation is good for — all talk, no action."

If I acted this brashly to any other Sergeant on any other fleet, heated words would have been exchanged (and potentially worse things), but not from the leader of the Crimson Tide. He doesn't get goaded into such trivial arguments. Instead, the man I could loosely call a father, not that I ever would, looks me dead in the eye with his even and calm persona.

"Yes, it's true that the Federation has been monitoring activity on RG-87 for about a year, but the planet is an unclaimed and unmarked territory on this side of the galaxy," he tells me in an even tone, attempting to disprove my argument. "Therefore, as silly as it sounds to you, Uuziks being on that planet is not a crime. We have no right to go searching random Uuziks, engaging in a hunt for their leader. That would be a war crime just as big as any Uuzik leader has committed. Unless we have definitive proof, none of which has been brought to my attention, then the Federation has no jurisdiction to simply land and overrun them. That's why we're allowing the Summit's fleet to keep tabs on the Uuziks' activities and make sure nothing happens. The only reason we're here is because over the past few days, there have been reports that the planet's condition is getting worse, and the Summit's fleet announced one of their soldiers had gone missing and most likely died in his exploration. We came to provide assistance. Once we arrived, though, the beacon started to go off and we rushed to the surface to help. However, instead, what we found was you."

He takes a long, drawn-out pause, his face becoming a bit more somber. "Now I know that you and the Federation have had your differences over the years," the Sergeant says looking down, hesitating with his words. This is a rare, if not unheard of, sight from the leader of the Crimson Tide.

"Rimor," he begins again. "How did you get your hands on that beacon?"

I roll my eyes in response to his dramatic reaction. I know what he's insinuating. In a way, it's kind of insulting that he'd think such absurd thoughts, but I guess when you live the life of a mercenary, it's only fair to assume they'll do whatever is required to ensure their mission's success. In a sense, he has a right to expect the worst from me, but at least this time, I can actually assure him.

"Relax," I say to him. "I didn't kill any of the Summit's men, or anyone else who's a part of the Federation, for that matter. As long as your men aren't hunting me, I have no reason to hunt them." I can see the fear disappear from the Sergeants face. "That solider was long done in by the Uuziks before I found his body."

I'll admit that I could break the news of a Federation death with a little more grace, but after being accused of the murder itself, I don't care much for the semantics. We still had bigger fish to fry. My focus remains on those who are still living and in immediate danger. Saving them is far more important than lingering in the past.

After more of this awkward exchange, I decide to get right to the point.

"Look, I appreciate you saving my ass down there, but since you just arrived on the scene and it's clear that the Summit's fleet isn't doing anything moderately close to a competent investigation, let me fill you in on the little slice of hell developing as we speak."

The Sergeant pays no mind to my less-than-subtle shot at his fellow Federation members, and instead he nods for me to proceed.

"While I was exploring RG-87 for materials, the Uuziks found my ship and set off explosives to destroy it. Since I was stranded with limited oxygen, I followed them back to their base and infiltrated it. I was looking for a ship, but I found far more interesting things along the way. Turns out the Uuziks are doing a bit more than you guys thought and are slowly draining the planet of all its life to build some sort of monstrous bioweapon. At any moment, this thing could be ready, and if its power is anywhere near what I've seen so far, then the Federation is going to regret not acting. Not only that, but millions of innocent lives will be wiped out. The same lives you are sworn to protect, if I recall."

"Monstrous bioweapon?" The Sergeant stares at me incredulously. "Surly if that were the case, we'd have got word from the Summit fleet by now. What proof do you have of this?"

I groan, really wanting to smack some sense into the man who considers himself my father.

"You mean besides seeing all this with my own eyes? Unlike your teams who sit and do nothing but watch, I actually broke into their base, read their logs, saw the research notes, and fought their twisted other experiments along the way. They plan to create this planet-obliterating monster that can bury itself underneath the planet's surface and harvest energy until it gains enough power to wipe out who knows what. And it won't just stop at one planet. They're engineering this thing so that after it runs out of energy, it will revert back to an egg state and go into hibernation so that they can start the process all over again!"

I can feel my blood boiling as I try to explain the situation. This is absurd, actually. I have no desire for Federation help, and they wouldn't do anything regardless. That is, assuming that they even believe my story. I continue. "So if you don't mind, I'm going back down to whatever remains of that planet, and I'm going to kill that weapon before it can do any more damage."

Hearing my impassioned, foreboding words would make any leader sweat, but not Sergeant Rupert Falcon Scott. He looks at me with a familiar stoic stare before opening his mouth to calmly express his opinion.

"And how do you plan to stop this weapon by yourself, may I ask? The last time you went searching their base, they nearly killed you, correct? Now you have no weapons, your Dynex suit has sustained incredible amounts of damage, and frankly, the fact that it still functions at all should be considered a miracle in its own right." His tone becomes a hair sharper, the way he would scold me if I were still a child. "But not only those things, you also don't know where or what it is you're actually up against. Because if that's your plan, then at least let me know ahead of time so that I can prepare my men to come save your ass again!"

This might be the most emotion I've heard in the Sergeant's voice in half a decade. But as much as I hate to admit it, he does have a point.

When you consider the mission for Calax Crystals to be a massive failure, which I do, on top of me escaping death only because of a mix of good fortune and dumb luck, my haste might be flawed. Also, this really has nothing to do with me anymore. I could get a ship and leave, never to think of RG-87 again. The Federation could deal with it—hey, that's what they're supposed to do, right? But I know I can't do that. Frankly, I don't trust the Federation not to get us all killed in their rule-abiding, procedurally run process.

A long pause follows the heated exchange. After the Sergeant takes a few breaths, he begins to talk in a tone more befitting of his role. "Will you just slow down for once in your life and let us make a plan? Let the Federation help you. Do that for me, and perhaps I'll overlook the Calax Crystals we found in your suit."

I nearly shoot out of my seat. "You went through my suit?!" But as soon as the words come out, I sit back down. After all, how shocked could I really be? The Federation has been interested in my suit for years, just like everyone else.

I begin to mull the offer over.

"Let's be clear. I'm not part of any Federation teams, and I'm sure as hell not rejoining the Federation after this. Your men can deal with the Uuziks on the surface, but I have a score to settle with their leader. Once that's done, I'll deal with this planet-killing monster. Got it?"

"All right, but you better not go dying on me this time. Understood?"

I stand up with a very slight half-smile. "Don't worry, I won't."

The Sergeant nods and stands up as well.

"Give me two hours to put a team together and brief everyone on the plan. Will that be good enough? Or is that considered wasting too much time for your liking?"

Everyone who's ever spoken to me about the Sergeant praises him as a man of integrity, honesty, and always with a cool and calm presence, but damn does he know how to needle me when he wants to.

I reluctantly agree to his timeframe. As far as I'm concerned, two hours is a miracle in and of itself. Based on Federation standards, I would've figured at least a few days, and even that I knew I'd have to accept. I can tell my warnings are being taken seriously.

I prepare to walk out, but before I can do so the Sergeant stops me again.

"Oh—I almost forgot something." His voice has a bit more life to it now. I turn around as he walks past me, gesturing for me to follow. He opens the door and looks back at me, "Come on, you're gonna want to see this."

I look at him wearily but decide to play along.

Down the hall and around a couple of corners, he opens up one of the metallic doors to the soldiers' suites. He knows I'm not about to take a nap, so I really have no clue why he's bringing me here.

Compared to the Sergeant's suite and, frankly, most of the ship, the soldiers' quarters are less than luxurious. And that's being polite. But considering how little time soldiers actually spend in these rooms, nobody ever really complains.

"While you were being pumped with oxygen, I had our technician team clean up your suit a little bit. Like I said, it was in awful shape when we found you."

We walk into the room, and all the beds are sticking out along the walls. And there, in the middle of the room hanging off a plastic mould in the shape of a human body, is my Dynex suit.

The paint has a fresh, metallic black and green gleam that lights up the room. Considering the damage sustained and the awful shape I'd left it in, if I didn't know any better, I'd think it was a brand-new suit. But I can still see some of the marks on the legs and arms of the metal. One, in particular, from a certain treklet's bite. That battle scar will remain for as long as I keep the suit, of that I'm certain.

Normally, I'd never let the Federation touch my suit. Or anyone else, for that matter. But especially not the Federation.

Ever since I first donned the one-of-a-kind tech suit three years ago, the Federation has carried keen interest in its technology. Of course, they know that I'll be the last person to help them learn about my suit, but what they and even I never expected was that the Bacardi apparently didn't hold the Federation in high enough regard to help them either. Every deal the Feds made, the Bacardi rejected in seconds.

See, the Bacardi are a bit of a different race on more than a few fronts. If you put aside their leading minds of research and development, they're not part of the Federation's jurisdiction, and they're one of only a dozen or so planets to live in such a manner, I'd say. Perhaps that's why I like working with them so much.

They formed their own government centuries before the Federation existed, they were well accustomed to their own rules and laws, but, most importantly, without the signing of the Federation's Peace Treaty, they're under no obligation to turn over their technology for Federation help.

On the other hand, if a planet or group decided they

were to attack the Bacardi and JE-11 in general, then likewise the Federation would have no obligation to come and support them. Not that attacking a planet with the most advanced technology to ever exist would be wise, but that's neither here nor there.

Obviously, they granted me the luxury of using their technology for a variety of reasons, and saving their president definitely played a big part in that. But I also believe part of the reason is because their government knew of my disdain for the Federation. They could be confident that I'd never turn over their secrets.

Even so, I have to give the Sergeant's crew some credit. They did a good job of cleaning things up. Besides, there's no way that they had enough time to learn such intricate machinery. So neither I nor the Bacardi have anything serious to worry about.

The Sergeant notices my trepidation and says, "I promise we didn't change a thing. You have my word as the Sergeant of the Crimson Tide."

Not taking his word as gospel, I stride past him and up to my suit. At a glance it looks good, but when it comes to my baby, I'm extremely particular.

Paranoia is top of the list of traits for a mercenary, even when it comes to a man who acted as if he was my own father. Instead of immediately believing him, I do a circle around the stand, examining every inch of the metal from top to bottom. I trust the Sergeant when he says they didn't fiddle with anything, but what I really want to make sure of is that there are no silly Federation marks stamped on it. Under the arms, on the back, behind the kneecaps…I check every inch of my suit. Once

I'm satisfied, I move on to the next test. Aesthetics are nice, but how does it feel once I step into it?

I pluck the chrome-green helmet off the exoskeleton and gaze into the visor. I see my own face staring back at me, and it's a mug so close to the verge of death that it's painful. But one with a growing smile of approval, as well.

Finally, I take the plunge and open up the back of the suit. When I enter and hear the familiar clicks of the back shutting, I put my helmet on and complete the set-up. Once my helmet touches the nape of the suit, the sounds similar to a computer booting up begin to ring in my ears. I can see though the replaced visor, and all my information starts scrolling down the left side, along with far more complex info and intel.

A big, big part of me hates to admit it because of how low the Federation can be, but in this case, they were true to their word and didn't mess with my suit in any respect. It's great, light, and agile, but still with the same powerful feel as before when I clench my fist.

When I turn around, the Sergeant looks back at me smugly. "So, good as new?"

"It's all right," I respond, deadpan. I have no intention of giving the Federation any credit.

"Right, then. You will also find you have a new photon sword in your wrist compartment. However, I did make my team take the liberty of infusing it into the suit, so you don't have to worry about losing this one."

I look at my wrist for a moment, then hold my arm out and give a thought-provoked, silent command. What shoots out is an almost translucent blue sword that causes the air around it to dance. It extends from my wrist like a long claw, meaning that I no longer have to attach my sword to my suit before a mission. I'll admit that the ease of use is pretty cool, and I want to know what sort of technology the Federation has been working on in secret to pull off such a feat. Are they trying to surpass the Bacardi in their advances? Because if they are, then all I can say is good luck on that one.

I turn to the Sergeant, and with as much sincerity as I can possibly muster, I say, "Thank you."

"You're welcome. Now, with that settled, let me gather our strike force. Meet me on the bow of the ship in a few hours."

And with that, the Sergeant left me — newly refurbished suit and all — to await his eventual command.

Time couldn't be moving any slower than if I was still sitting back on that ball of dirt waiting for my oxygen to run out.

I guess, in one sense, that can be seen as a positive. It means that we aren't wasting as much time as the Federation usually would when preparing for a mission. On the other hand, not knowing how much time we have, each passing second is agonizing. Outside the long, glass window floats that depressing, decaying planet.

In all honesty, I'm not even sure how much I care about saving the planet. In fact, the planet is a lost cause. The damage sustained can't be reversed, and win or lose, it'll be uninhabitable in short order. I certainly don't care much for helping keep the Federation from being destroyed, either. Obviously, it would have big consequences if something that catastrophic were to happen, but I'd manage.

What I really want, more than anything, is to stick it to those Uuziks. That's why I'm so hellbent on being the one to take down Fenrich, his top-secret weapon, and that group of monsters who've taken so much from me — the chance to know my family and the potential of an entirely different life in which I'm not the subject of so many miserable childhood memories. Perhaps I wouldn't have ever become a mercenary at all.

Revenge is what I want. Ever since growing up, all my life I've been scared of the Uuziks, worried that the power-hungry monsters will come back for me. But now I've taken their best shot, surviving on multiple occasions, and with the cards constantly stacked against me. This time will be different. I have no need to be scared, and I have nothing to fear.

With that in mind, I'm ready to finish what I started. Too bad I made an agreement with the Sergeant. I stand pat, waiting for the green light just like everyone else.

I know it's for good reason. If I'm to pull this off, I need a fair deck of cards, if not one that's slightly stacked in my favour. My limits are plainly obvious at this point, and going back into the hornet's nest alone would be a suicide mission. Even mercenaries have to accept such a fate sometimes.

When I look at RG-87, even with a passing glance, I can tell that the planet is hanging by a thread. With the storm clouds surrounding it and the deathly sick atmosphere growing bigger by the day, my patience is being tested.

There's a nice alcove on the second floor of the Crimson Tide that I spent many hours sleeping in as a teen. It's just big enough for me to fit inside, and I'm able to stretch my legs while sitting back comfortably. The best part is that nobody knows it exists, and one is well out of sight while sitting in it. I'd come hide here whenever I was angry and needed to blow off some steam or when the Sergeant yelled at me for messing up in training. It might be the only place on this giant ship that brings me comfort. Normally, I can put my feet up and chill before a mission with ease, but this time I can barely sit still.

An hour or so later I finally hear a message over the loudspeakers.

"RG-87 Task Force, please report to the main deck. I repeat, RG-87 Task Force, and that means you, Rimor..."

I roll my eyes before making my way to the main deck. All of this is just going to be a formality for me.

On the main deck of the ship are rows of men and women lined up in an orderly fashion. With their copy-and-paste Federation uniforms, they resemble an army of clones. I don't care to count, but there must be well over a hundred soldiers standing and saluting.

I begin walking down the stairs, aware that I'm a bit late. When the Sergeant said he was going to put a team together, I didn't think he meant an army. I guess when it comes to the Uuziks, the Federation shows some guts.

The Sergeant stands in front of his troops with his back to me. To make sure nobody confuses me with a Federation soldier, I remain leaning up against the back wall. It's not like I need to listen to the man's speech anyway.

Yes, technically I'm part of the mission, but we both know his instructions mean nothing to me. I have my own solo mission, and the Sergeant has accepted that.

And even if he'd been against it, as long as I'm the only one with a Dynex suit, I remain the only one properly equipped to fight the destructive Project BB.

Paying more attention to my own thoughts and my own gameplan rather than the Sergeant's less-than-riveting brief, I catch a glimpse of him turning around to eye me. He definitely made mention of me in some regard, but I wasn't paying enough attention to catch what it was. I opt to remain stoic and stare straight ahead while he turns his back to me once again.

"All right, soldiers—get ready to move out. Time is of the essence here, but as long as you remember your roles, do your job, and trust in your fellow soldier, this mission will be a success. And, most importantly, as long as everyone comes back alive. Do I make myself clear?"

Finally, something that's relevant to me. It's go time.

Troops begin storming the docking bay of the Crimson Tide, mobilizing into small groups and entering their ships. Most of these are much higher-quality space crafts than mine, but they lack subtlety to them, not that it matters. I say, let the Uuziks know we're coming. Let them be scared.

Of course, that means that if the Uuziks are making preparations for our arrival, they might be able to pick off more people than they otherwise would with one-man army ships (as I like to call them), but this way, the Federation can also get more troops at different parts of the base in wide numbers.

The Uuziks have been on high alert the second they learned of my survival, but once I managed my escape, it's hard to say what they believe happened to me. They might think I'm dead, or perhaps still roaming the planet, but I don't picture them expecting a miraculous escape. Though if they assume the latter, this could be even more dangerous than people expect.

I follow up with Sergeant Scott and he directs me to a simplistic, one-man army ship sitting on the runway. He salutes me, and since he stayed true to his word, I reciprocate the gesture.

Now in the ship, I set course and wait for clearance as larger vessels continue to spit out from the mouth of the Crimson Tide. They soon become small snowflakes in the darkness of space.

Plummeting down to the surface once again, this time I land only a rock's skip away from the Uuzik base. My plan of attack really has no tactical strategy. The reason I'm deployed so close to last is because any thoughts of stealth are out the window. I'll be making my entrance with a bang.

The landing is rocky, but I ignore it. I hop out of my ship and find myself right in the middle of a firefight.

I land near the front-left part of the base, and I see about 20 Federation soldiers sending return fire to a dozen Uuziks attempting to hold the front door. The other units are surrounding the base, and even a few are coming through the rooftop. Every inch of this base will be surrounded by Feds in minutes.

Blasters fire back and forth, and alarms that sound all too familiar blare across the planet. The entire scene turns into a warzone, and I'm running headfirst into the middle of it.

Even though I hate the Federation and their silly processes, I do know from firsthand experience that all their ranks are well-trained and can fight with gusto. This time, we also have the advantage of sheer numbers. The soldiers are overwhelming the Uuziks faster than I could have imagined.

Wave after wave, the power-hungry race of monsters march to their deaths. Fenrich cares little about sending so many to be his meat shields, of that I'm confident. You'd almost feel bad if they didn't have it coming.

Before long, the Uuziks are overrun and on the retreat. If they can close the doors to their steel fortress, at least they'd have some time to regroup. It's also possible they want to funnel us in to make picking us off much easier. I expect Fenrich to make an appearance at any time, but he fails to show thus far. I have a feeling I know where he is, though.

The doors begin a slow groan as they inch together, but when a quarter of the way closed, two spider-like webs zoom past me and latch onto the edges of each door. Sparks flicker out from these webs, and the doors light up before ceasing to function. Then, like a jailbreak, men and women from the Federation pour through them, guns blazing.

I lead the charge, and my freshly restored Dynex suit is a shield to any oncoming blaster bullets. They clanked off my satisfying defense, and I take out the half-dozen Uuziks on the far side of the warehouse.

Unlike the last few times I ran through here, a significant light shines in. Bathed in yellow, the whole room has a new perspective, and one far more horrid than I first imagined.

I've seen my fair share of warzone planets, but this place is on another level. Bodies of Uuziks are splattered on the floor with blaster holes in various places, loose wires hang from the crumbling ceiling, and fiery sparks shoot from overhead and in every possible direction.

For a moment, I figure the Federation is the cause of so much damage, but on second thought, I realize that it's just a desperate ploy by the Uuziks. They'd rather collapse the entire warehouse in on itself than let the Federation further into the base, but the plan backfires.

I step back as everyone pours through the first door like a rushing torrent. My logic in staying back comes from knowing how slippery the Uuziks can be. Federation soldiers could be (and, more importantly, should be) able to handle any threats they're prepared for, but I want to stay back and help out if any lingering peril comes from behind. At least this way, I can prevent any sneak attacks.

Helping the Federation isn't in my plans, but the last thing I want is someone else, Federation soldier or not, dying at the hands of these Uuziks.

Once I'm fairly certain that there's no incoming danger, I follow up the rear and make my way to the main base's cylindrical tower. The red flashing lights and sirens bellow out from every directions. I ignore all such alarms this time.

More shots fire from above as the Uuziks prepare an aerial assault. They're scaling the walls, climbing downwards, and filling up every doorway.

But the Sergeant's crew keeps their composure and does what's necessary to contain the threats.

I storm through with a small group of soldiers across the bridge, and we begin making our way down to the basement floors. Charging into a top-secret base is much easier when you can throw caution to the wind.

The Sergeant and the rest of his army are scaling the

upper floors of the fortress, ransacking the place and taking no prisoners. This is not at all the style of the Federation, which almost always refuses to shoot first. But when it comes to the Uuziks, all bets are off. Besides, even the Uuziks would rather die than be taken in by the Federation. They'd turn any negotiations into a fight to the death.

We blow the doors open with ease but are met with blaster shots screaming down on us.

This is one of the scenarios I was most worried about. If Project BB is as close to fruition as I fear and as their logs predict, there's a chance it will become Fenrich's top priority. Knowing him, he'd send waves of disposable minions — which, for the Uuziks, means everyone — but it also means that we might be seriously outnumbered below.

I take charge, knowing that my suit can handle more damage than an average Federation uniform. I run through the door and flip a table over for cover. Crouching down, I blindly return fire before seeing a small round object, similar to a tennis ball, fly over my head and into the middle of the room. A loud bang echoes, along with a flash of blinding lights.

I pop my head up and take out two Uuziks side by side, while the rest of my group storms in and finishes the job. With only one Uuzik left, who's also charging toward me, I activate my new photon sword. One clean swing chops the monster in half, leaving it in a pile of blood and gore.

Typically, I'd call that excessive force and a waste of energy, but I really want to try out my new weapon. Well, between the destruction of my planet and the multiple attempts on my life, maybe it isn't overkill enough.

I follow the route from memory then enter the elevator.

Next stop: the depths. I gesture for the soldiers to secure the area, and I make sure nobody interferes with the second part of my mission.

Running through the disgusting, disheveled basement (which was previously my temporary grave), my fists tighten. I hate being back here, but this time I'm in a far better position. I'm not worried about my oxygen, my blaster and photon sword are at the ready, and I've got a little added secret weapon on my side. I follow my map through the dreaded sewers, looking for that slight turn off that leads even further down into RG-87.

Water drips down all around me and rats are scurrying everywhere — at least I think they are. My mind might be playing tricks on me. Silence can do that to you, especially when you know there's an all-out war going on a few floors above.

It's strange — the further down I go, all those sound… the blasters, the ringing of the alarms…they all disappear into the background.

I take the next turn and find the sealed-off door. When I double check my map, it confirms that this is the place, the path that will lead me even further below. The seal looks fresh, perhaps put into place by the tyrant leader himself.

My sword jets out and I jam it into the heart of the door before lifting upward. I slice it up and down furiously before finally ripping it open. I have to admit that the new blade is far stronger than the little butter knife of a sword I was using before. I kick out the center of the door, but as I do I hear the monstrous footsteps of an evil presence coming from behind.

Only one Uuzik has such an intimidating stomp.

Despite the tyrant coming my way, I still have the option to run. I could dart through this shredded door and make a straight shot for the depths.

But I ignore the opportunity. First of all, I'd be followed, and there's no doubt about that. Secondly, I think it's clear that I have a bone to pick with this tyrant.

I hold my sword out in front of my body as Fenrich comes into view. The dull lights hanging along the walls do little for my sight, but the power of my glowing sword is more than enough to see my opponent. Our arena will be the long, concrete hallway deep underneath the Uuzik base.

"You have courage, Merc," he says in his disgusting voice. "Not many would dare return to the sight of their grave after escaping death the way you did. You could've left freely, gone into hiding, never to be spotted again. But instead, you choose to return and fight alongside those Federation dogs." He brandishes his long, double-bladed axe, and it gleams from the light of my sword.

"What can I say — I still have some unfinished business. After all, we never did get to finish our duel. You claim that 'the Uuzik way' is built around power, so here's your chance to prove it. If you kill me now, you can still save your precious weapon and ultimately take control of the universe. But if you lose…well, I think you can figure out the rest. No Federation interference, no Uuziks jumping in, no giant bone dragon. Just me and you."

"You know something, Merc? I like your attitude. I guess I shouldn't be surprised, though. Eluding me and my men for as long as you have while being under our noses the entire time is no easy feat. But before we start, I'd like to make you an offer. You understand how much we Uuziks appreciate strength more than anything else, and we can use a man of your talents. It will pay handsomely. All you have to do is help me rid this planet of the Federation."

Thankfully, the lower part of my visor covers up my mouth, curling in disgust. I can't believe what I've just heard. Did the leader of the Uuziks actually just try to recruit me, moments before I plan to kill him? It's a trap. It has to be a trap. He'd kill me just as he'd killed his own men before, and then the Federation would be gone. And, not long after, so would I.

But Fenrich drops his guard when he places the head of his axe on the ground in a display of honesty. I'm starting to believe him. Uuziks aren't tied to their race—they're tied to their beliefs. If I believe what they believe and fall in line, then I probably could work alongside them.

However, our ideals would never line up. I'd never attempt to dominate, sell, and destroy planets for selfish gain.

I glare at my enemy. "First, let me ask you a question. Does the planet AR-337 ring a bell?"

The tyrant stares at me with his caved in eyes, his face contorting in thought.

Instead of waiting for an answer, I decide to help jog his memory.

"It was 17 years ago when you and your gang of thugs landed on that planet and slaughtered every last person while stealing the planet's resources. You killed billions and left the planet in ruins."

"AR-337? It doesn't sound familiar. No, wait—it was that ball of dirt with the tremendous amount of water on it, yes? I do remember. We sold that planet for a bountiful profit. And all it took was removing the pitiful race that occupied it — Earthlings. Such a weak species, hardly worth keeping alive. Although perhaps they would have made good slaves…"

I'm enraged. "Weak race? My race was peaceful and nurturing, and they helped each other and every other race all over the galaxy! Maybe we weren't perfect all the time, but we were the farthest thing from weak!"

"It was a species that had no true leader. A species that fought amongst each other over the most trivial aspects of life. I studied your planet before our mission. They were anything but peaceful or nurturing. But it doesn't matter now. They're all gone, as all pitiful races are doomed to be. Gone."

"All except for one, because on that day, you made one fatal mistake."

"Oh, and that would be?"

"In your power-hungry extermination efforts, you left one small child behind. He survived. And that child is about to make you pay for your arrogance."

Venom drips from my words as I lunge forward, my photon blade jetting out. I open with a high swing over my head, ready to chop down on the tyrant leader, but he lifts his axe and blocks me flush. I spring back as he swings in a wide horizontal arc.

"I'm going to make you regret the day you let me live. I can promise you that!" I make a second charge at the monster, hacking with all my strength. Though we've fought briefly before, it wasn't enough for me to pick up any discernible patterns of his. It's obvious how much of his life he's spent training with that axe, though, because he easily blocks my slashes and counter attacks.

He deflects my ferocious slash, and then with a wild, expansive arc swing, he nearly cuts me in half.

I manage to step back, feeling the ripple of the wind impale my stomach as the blade flies by. Even a freshly restored Dynex suit won't hold up against a direct slash of his axe. It might not break clean through, but it would doubtless leave a nasty gash.

As a big bruiser, I think that speed will be my best advantage. I bait him into an attack; he drops his axe like an anvil into the ground, shaking the very foundation of RG-87. I roll past him and shoot forward with my blade pointing true. There's now a small gap in his armour. But before I get close enough, he sticks his long arm out and manages to grab me by my face mask. Before I can cut myself loose, he throws me into the stone wall. I crash against the rock feeling the bones in my back rattling from impact. The tyrant remains relentless, charging at me with his axe scraping along the ground.

He prepares for an upper cut and then thrusts his axe, but it smashes into the wall, and the rock shatters as I roll out of the way. I get to my feet, and with enough distance between us, I pull out my pistol and take three shots to his chest. They bounce off his plated armour with a ting, and he smiles menacingly at me.

"If you plan to live up to your promise, you'll have to do better than measly blaster shots."

"Oh, don't worry—that's far from all I have."

I know he's right. My pistol will do little to hurt him as

long as his body remains clad in that black armour. And I'm not even confident my sword can penetrate the metal. No doubt that it was built from some of the most durable materials in the galaxy.

Fenrich keeps at his relentless assault while brandishing an angry smile of pure, evil joy. The thrill of battle pumps his blood in the way it does for all Uuziks.

He drops his battle axe on me from high above like a guillotine chop, but I block it just in the nick of time. He refuses to let up, continuing to push the full weight of his attack down on me. My legs are beginning to buckle, and I grip my left arm with my right to hold position. We lock hilts and come in close.

"You are indeed a worthy opponent. I'm glad my men didn't kill you that day on AR - 337. I would've never been granted such a worthy battle."

I growl at his words. They're honest words, but at the expense of my planet, they feel like mockery. I push him back and we release, ready to duel again.

Nobody can question Fenrich's pure strength, but that alone isn't what makes him so dangerous. He has the training and skill to back up such power. For a creature of his size, his agility and mobility are impeccable. I've even been using my thrusters to provide a little added speed, and still he keeps up with my every move.

He might be one of the most powerful entities in the entire galaxy. From what I've seen in my life, it can easily be argued that he's actually the most powerful.

Explosive sparks shoot from our weapons with each swing. I want to slay this beast that ravaged my planet, put me through the hell that he created, and avenge the lives he's taken. But now I can't help but wonder if I'll come to realize that I've perhaps made a mistake.

I'd escaped his clutches not once, but twice before, and maybe for him the third time would be the charm. Should I have brought the Sergeant along? Or tried to overrun him with Federation soldiers? If I die here and Fenrich manages to unleash his experiment, then my arrogance and lust for vengeance could end the rest of the universe as we know it.

I glare at the monster across from me, both of us breathing heavy. He relaxes his stance and speaks.

"I hate to see such strength go to waste, but when you challenge an Uuzik to battle, you guarantee that one of us will be slain before it ends."

"If it's to the death you want, then I'll have to make sure it's your death!" I mock his words, but my confidence is dwindling.

I do have a plan in mind, although one could call it more of a prayer. Up close, I can now see a few small openings near Fenrich's lower hips. Those gaps in the armour are my target.

We clash again and lock horns, but this time I drop my support hand, feeling his axe dip closer to my mask. I manage to hold steadfast just long enough to enact my strategy.

With one fluid motion, I pull out my pistol for a second attempt. But this time, I'm close enough to shoot him in those tiny openings on his hips.

I pull the trigger, and the reaction from Fenrich is instantaneous. A low rumbling groan escapes from his lips and I can feel the gravity of his axe loosen. I push the axe high into the sky and slice at his chest with as much vigor as I can manage.

But just as I'd feared, my blade can't piece through his armour.

He roars louder and stumbles back before regaining his composure. Perhaps it's only a stunning blow, but the large gash across his chest suggests that maybe it accomplishes more than I'd thought.

I bide my time, not wanting to rush the moment. I've finally inflicted damage, but by no means will this be enough to stop such a monster.

Enraged, Fenrich charges toward me with more speed than I expect. I block his swing, but he strikes me so hard that I fly back. I smash my head against the stone wall again, crumpling over and feeling rubble falling upon my head. My body rattles around in my suit from the bone-jarring hit, but I force myself up. My adrenaline pumps through my veins, negating any pain I otherwise should be feeling.

Fenrich charges at me again, his logic and strategy fading. I manage to evade his violent provocation, landing another precise swing to his chest. This time, he looks visibly wounded, staggering backwards before regaining his balance.

We both stop to catch our breaths. I've all but forgotten that there's a war taking place between the Uuziks and the Federation only a few floors above me. The only thing on my mind is killing Fenrich.

"You're a slippery one, Merc. It's been ages since I've felt my own blood. No wonder you eluded my men for so long—none of them have the tenacity and skill you've displayed. However, as long as you choose to stand in the way of our plans and fight alongside those Federation dogs, I'll be forced to cut you down where you stand. It's nothing personal. But I guess as a merc, nothing's personal to you, is it?"

"Don't you worry—this is very personal. You killed my family, ravaged my home planet, and destroyed a race of innocent people. I won't let you get away with that ever again."

I charge. Flames of rage burn inside me, and with them come my second wind. We exchange blows, and I can tell that he's weakening from the gash in his chest. But it isn't enough. I need something more. Some kind of a deciding factor to beat him and his Calax Crystal-absorbing monster…

And then it occurs to me. The remaining Calax Crystal. He'd never expect it. A plan so risky would bring his previous statement true for certain: One of us will die in the end.

I shove him back to get some distance between us. I hold my left hand in the air and watch the Uuzik tyrant's face contort with strange confusion.

The compartment in my arm slides open, and out springs a tiny Calax Crystal, the only remaining one from my hellish journey. As the gem floats down, a glint of its white light catches Fenrich's eye. His mouth twitches.

I snatch the stone out of the air and smirk. "Did I just see Fenrich, leader of the Uuziks, flinch in the face of a fight?"

"You wouldn't dare. You saw what such power did to your weapon the last time you used it. A Calax Crystal would only lead to your death. It's a foolish mistake to make."

"Only one way to find out, I guess." I smile smugly, but I know that he has a point. This plan could backfire. But for some reason I can't explain, I know that it won't.

The only remaining hope I have is an extremely tiny one.

Compared to the crystal I put in my blaster—or worse, in my suit—this one is easily four or five times smaller. This is only a sliver of power, but it's still plenty of punch to sway the tides of my battle. I was hoping to save it for the monster stewing about below, but I need to live long enough in order to see that first.

I pop the crystal into my other arm's compartment and feel the heat envelop my body once again. But this one pales in comparison to the last two times. I also make sure to keep the exuberant power source in conjunction with my sword, meaning that if it blows a fuse, the rest of my suit will still function. At least I hope it will.

The lights of my sword start to sputter and flicker until they turn into dancing flames. The fast-acting crystal grows my sword twice as large as it was, but it strangely feels lighter.

I glare at Fenrich and swing my sword through the air a few times, smirking. "Yeah, this will do just fine. You ready, Fenrich? Because this is where your reign of terror ends!"

With my new and blessed power, I dash forward like I'm shot out of cannon. Based on both previous uses of this tremendous power, I know it's far from sustainable. I need to act quickly and be decisive in order to pull this off.

I swing with the force and anger of anyone and everyone who's ever died at the hands of this monster, relentlessly pushing Fenrich back each time our weapons clash.

"You dare speak that way to the Lord of the Uuziks? Mark my words, you will lay dead at my feet, Merc!"

"As long as I live, I won't let you or your clan hurt anyone else. I won't let you ruin any more families or destroy any more planets. This is your end, Fenrich!"

I lunge forward for my final strike, and so does he. Only this time, his speed and agility can't compare with mine. We stand in a perfect pose, his large body towering over mine in a freeze frame. His axe is wrapped tightly under my arm; he missed from striking me clean in the chest by a mere fraction.

I, however, strike true, finally breaking through his thick, armored skin. My Calax-infused blade pierces his chest and protrudes out the other side, leaving him lifeless as his heart bleeds out.

His disgusting, glossy eyes, now devoid of life, stare vacantly ahead as he falls toward me. My sword dematerializes, and I take a step to my right.

He collapses to the ground. I win the fight. I finally get the revenge I desired for so, so very long.

"That…is for my planet…" I grunt through deep, well-earned, exhaustive breaths.

Sadly, there's no time to rejoice in my achievement. I still have another mission to complete.

Fenrich, the Uuzik leader, died by my sword, and that's a massive blow to the Uuzik forces. But I know the way of the Uuziks well enough to realize that it won't end with him. They'll bring on a new leader and regroup on their home planet. While they do that, I want to make sure it won't be with the destructive power they're cultivating below.

I check my suit and my sword, and I realize they've endured the energy of the Calax Crystal quite well. Perhaps the Bacardi can make the overpowered gem work one day after all. I can't even imagine the possible power that it could wield.

These are thoughts that can be expanded upon later, though.

I walk into the same room I entered before Fenrich arrived, fully prepared for what will come next.

Although, to call this a room would be a sizable exaggeration. It's nothing more than an elevator-sized box. I move straight ahead into a second room that's the exact same size, but this one has a button on its end wall. I give it a tap and watch the red light brighten. Based on my map, this should lead me to the lair of Project BB.

I stand there in the one-person pod, wondering what could possibly lay below me. It's not like I have much to go off of — just a few grainy photos with details I couldn't even make out, and an unfortunately drawn Uuzik rendition of a black egg.

Jets boot up around me, and then my body goes weightless for a second. My heart leaps into my throat as flashbacks of the free-falling incident from the top of the spire play in my mind. Thankfully it's nothing to fear, and the pod shoots down quickly. When it lands with a thud, I hear a small ding and the door pops open. Before I step out and see where the pod has taken me, I can feel an invisible force hitting my face. A chaotic energy courses through the air, creating a thick muggy atmosphere that I can barely breath in. The energy remains invisible, but, without question, something potent is lingering.

When I make my way out into the wide-open space, I'm absolutely blown away. Thousands of Calax Crystals are jetting out of the walls everywhere I look. Each one of them gleams and sparkles bright enough to illuminate the entire room.

On top of that, they're growing out of the cracks in the

bedrock like clumps of weeds. I'm walking on a gold mine, or, in this case, Calax Crystal mine of power.

Now I also understand what that heavy energy floating through the air is. The energy radiating off the glowing white crystals is palpable, and with so much of them in one area, I can taste its effects.

I move forward and nearly step in a puddle of Calax liquid. Faint smoke rises off of it, creating a burning and foul stench. After avoiding it, I make my way through the crystal-filled cave before stepping into a much wider room.

This is when I see one of the most disgusting things I've ever laid my eyes on. Toward the far end of the wall, hanging up dead center, is what can only be described as a giant egg sack. It's entirely black, but coated with some kind of a misty purple colour. I'll never forget such a repulsive sight, but not because the egg sack is odd and black and purple. It's because it's squirming. It looks as if there's a monster inside that could burst out at any moment, and I'm fairly sure that this is the case.

This disgusting, enormous cocoon takes up almost a third of the wall. It has lines like veins shooting out from every angle, going up and down the stone wall and around the entire room. They must be its roots, because they, like the egg itself, are pulsating with what I can only imagine to be nutrients from the Calax Crystals embedded in the bedrock.

I inch my way towards it, my guard at an all-time high. When I'm close, I can see that the egg sack isn't as big as I first thought. In fact, it's more like two parts—the first an egg sack that's maybe twice my size with something moving around in it, presumably absorbing the nutrients. The second part is what I believe to be the base of the sack, mutating into the wall like an infection spreading all over someone's body.

Time is running out, and I need to act quick if I'm going to stop whatever is growing inside.

The obvious solution for most people would be to simply walk up and stab the egg sack, hopefully killing the lifeform inside. But I'm not keen on such an idea. For one, I don't really want to get that close to it, and two, cutting into a pulsating sack is careless and potentially a really bad idea. I mean, who the hell knows what would happen if I cut the bloody thing open? Pandora's box of mayhem and horror, for all I know.

Hearing strange slurping sounds below me, I look down and realize I'm standing on one of its veins. Then I come up with my next move.

The safest bet in this scenario is to deal with the food supply of whatever beast is inside. With my trusty blade now back to normal and surviving the influx of power I'd granted it, I pick up this vein like a piece of slimy rope. Even through the sensors in my suit, I realize that it carries an electric energy to it. It barely lifts from the ground, having no slack in its line, but I still have enough room to slice the cord clean in half.

Both ends snap back, one flying into the bedrock, the other flying into the base of the wall where the egg hangs. Murky, blue liquid sprays everywhere, like a severed limb spewing blood.

Upon cutting one source of the egg's nutrients, something interesting happens. The pulsating and pumping sounds it emits increase like a quickening, feverish heartbeat.

I cut another line and the speed increases again. Each cut causes the sources of energy to reroute, making the other veins pulsate quicker and more noticeably. I hurry my pace, trying to cut the other lines in hopes of killing the beast inside before I'm forced into actually stabbing the egg. I really don't want to attempt such a questionable tactic.

But due to my haste, I fail to notice the furious sloshing sound in the sack has quickened. What I'm actually doing by cutting off the monster's food supply turns out to be nothing less than causing it to awaken from hibernation early.

After cutting a few more cords, the sloshing becomes so loud I can't ignore it anymore. Now I know I'm in for a real fight.

I cut the last cord and a shrieking cry fills the air, sending chills down my spine. The violent wail of pain makes me once again question my choice to come alone. It's one thing to settle a grudge with the Uuziks' leader, but battling this thing? I know I hate the Federation, but dying to whatever this creature is would be a fairly grotesque end.

The bedrock below my metal-suited feet begins to shake violently. The whole room quivers with rocks and crystals from the ceiling, dropping down and nearly crushing both myself and the egg.

But then a claw shoots out of the egg sack. It looks like the Uuziks' claws, but it's coated in black with neon white at the end. It also has a more considerable arc than Uuzik claws.

A second claw tears through the heart of the sack, just like the first. Both of them are as long as my body and are swinging back and forth, struggling to break the shell's skin.

Before I can decide my next move, the beast breaks free of its shell-shackle and emerges from the egg. Its body is midnight black, but each limb—just like its claws—has a translucent white light glowing on the inside. Calax Crystal liquid oozes and splashes on the ground, spilling out from the inside of the broken, disgusting cocoon.

I've spent so much time wondering, and now Project BB stands only a few dozen feet away from me. But I can still see the pointed, blood-red eyes on its oddly shaped head.

Its body is like a malformed spider, but with only four legs and a round body that's much further off the ground. This monster in front of me looks slightly different from the poor rendition I discovered in one of the Uuziks labs, but this is irrelevant. All I can hope for is that I woke it before it's reached maximum maturity. If I were to go up against the full power of such a potent, freakish beast, I'd be wiped away in a heartbeat.

Regardless, I'm in for the fight of my life, and with a creature formed by feeding off of what's likely the strongest energy source in the known galaxy.

I need to plot my next move. Thankfully, BB is simply looking around and making strange noises. It acts like a newborn, unsure of its whereabouts and still getting acclimated to its new freedom. It turns its head to stare at me, and once it does, I know it's time to move.

BB lets out a staggering roar before taking off and up the side of the wall after moving freely through the liquid splashed on the ground. I wait patiently, searching for my window. I want to see what will come of this creature's rampage.

I avoid any sudden movements while keeping my eyes fixated on the beast. It's already aware of me, but by no means does it show any interest. Not yet anyway. This is when I realize what its intentions are. Climbing the walls, it opens its elongated mouth and ingests the Calax Crystals whole. It crushes them with its giant pincer teeth and absorbs the nutrients required for it to function.

This tells me that I did cut off the food supply, and also that it indeed hasn't reached maturity yet.

But this means that I need to stop it now, before it gains the strength that I fear it will.

I pull out my pistol and open fire on the vermin, seeing if I can draw its attention away.

Before the blasts can strike BB's eye, it lifts a claw and tanks the hits with ease. For being a mindless monster, the newly hatched, terrifying being shows more smarts than I'd given it credit for.

The white spots on BB pulsate like electric transmissions, likely indicating that it has or is in the process of digesting the crystals.

Rushing to attack before BB can gain full power, I swing my sword with as much force as I can. It lifts its front-left claw and blocks my incoming assault. I hold my sword strong, pushing with all my might in hopes of cutting clean through the shell skin, but after a few seconds I can tell I'm making no headway.

I jump back when I see BB ready its right claw to swipe at me. I land hard, crashing into a Calax Crystal patch. After being pushed away, I expect BB to come at me with full force, but again it lets me be. Instead, it directs its attention to its food source along the other wall. Scurrying toward it, the monster clings onto each patch of Calax Crystals and absorbs them again.

I don't have much of a plan anymore. My futile efforts of

violent swings are doing nothing but bouncing off. I can't even move BB off its feeding spot, let alone hurt it.

Until its hunger has been satisfied, my life appears to be in no danger. But after that, I and everyone else on this planet will be obliterated. In order to win, I need more power. Unlike the tyrant's armour, this creature has no openings or gaps on its body.

I have to shatter his exterior if I'm to have any hope of killing this thing. Wait, I wonder if…

A horrible yet ingenious idea forms in my mind. One that should work in my favour, assuming it doesn't back-fire and cement my death for certain this time. And with the creature munching down on crystals, I even have time to pull it off.

Running over to the wall closest to me, the furthest one from BB, I saw off a clump of crystals. It has to be more than three times the size of any crystal I've ever used be-fore. I break off a second one, because in spite of its size, I know that one won't be enough.

I take the first one and place it in the slot attached to my photon sword, and the second one I embed into the chest of my suit's battery. Essentially, I'm making the de-cision to end our battle in short order. But the question remains — which of us will die?

Instantly, my body heats up with the tingling sensa-tion of raw power coursing through my blood. My body is sweltering, and my sword morphs back into a long blade of dancing flames. This is my trump card. Go all in, using as much power as possible. Once time runs out and the crystals' powers take their unrelenting with-drawal effects, it's all over with. Then again, if the choices are to either die by Calax Crystals or die by BB, I'll gladly choose the former.

I dash forward with blurring speed, and with my thrusters in overdrive, I move that much faster. I stab clean through BB's armour before it can react.

It lets out an enraged cry as I hold my blade firm, the blazing heat melting its insides. Then I rip it out and duck what would have been a killer swipe. I keep moving with top speed, giving BB no chance to keep up. Everywhere I move, I get in a few whacks at him, all with the hopes of so many lives on my back. Each slash sends chips of BB's armour flying off like shattered glass. I press on, ignoring my time limit. After a number of heavy hits, I finally see a significant crack run up the monster's left side and reach up across its eye and forehead. Finally, some progress.

The cracks becoming more significant, I catch a glimpse of some fleshy blue organ beating loudly. Thud after thud. It must be the creature's heart. If my suspicion is correct, then I have a small chance to inflict some real damage. I move in for the strike, but just like before, BB displays a level of intelligence I'm not expecting.

When I stab with a lateral thrust, the creature uses its claws to block the blue, beating organ. Thinking quickly and feeling the toll of the Calax Crystals on my body, I grab my gun. Practically ripping it out of the holster, I begin shooting at the monster's eyes. It has a decision to make—use its claws to protect its eyes, or remain steady and protect its heart, giving me free access to destroying its vital eyesight.

As anyone would, BB chooses to safeguard its heart, and my blasts strike true to its eyes. The monster groans in agony from each pull of my trigger, but refuses to grant me access to its weak point. That's entirely fine with me — I have other methods to make it flinch.

I jump high into the air and BB takes a free swing at me. I block the scythe claw, landing on the monster's head.

Like a knife through steaming, fresh bread, my sword jets into BB's eye socket, causing it to scream out in a high-pitched wail. The cries bounce off the bedrock, echoing out to the point that anyone within a hundred-mile radius can certainly hear it. There's no way it can resist opening up for me now.

With one ill-fated swing of its claw to push me out of its eye socket, I slide down the side and roll underneath it, its glowing blue heart directly in my line of vision. Another painstaking cry rings out as I jam my flaming sword into its heart, watching the blue glow turn to a hot white. I continue to swing in a high arc with as much force as anyone who despises the last 24 hours of his life could.

Swish.

The energy remaining from the Calax Crystals dwindle as I hammer the final nail in BB's coffin. Pushing up, I cut clean through its heart, body, and face. BB splits in half, with a glowing light coursing through its body before melting into a pile of ooze. Calax Crystal ooze.

The Uuziks' plan is foiled, and with all threats averted, I'm only left with one issue: the melting body of BB towering over top of me.

The remnants of liquid-infused Calax drench my suit and seep through the metal, making its way to my body. As it turns out, the intensity of using a crystal is nothing compared to the pain of having it drench your skin. My body burns like I'm being melted alive. I want to scream, but nothing escapes my lips minus an almost defeated breath. I roll back and forth in agony, begging for the pain to stop.

I don't know what happened next. I blacked out from the pain for an unknown amount of time. But when I wake up, I'm still face down in BB's bedrock graveyard. The pain has subsided, although now I feel like I'm in an eternal inferno — my body temperature is through the roof. Nothing physical stops me from standing up, and yet I can't. I'm pinned to the ground by my own fatigue.

After a few minutes of laying still, I hear a crashing sound, and then an unfamiliar noise. The ground starts to shake.

It can't be. That bastard tyrant can't still be alive.

I grip the bedrock with my fingers, but even that proves a herculean task. I hear a door slide open. Someone must have taken a pod down, the same way I did earlier…

I twist my head toward the sound, but all I see are a pair of white and black shoes approaching me. Thankfully, they're not Uuzik shoes, but Federation standard shoes. Not that I wish to be seen in such a sorry state by the Federation, but then again, they've already seen me on my deathbed once, so what's one more time? Besides, pride comes second to my survival, and right now I need help.

I hear somewhat of a condescending voice, and yet I've never been so glad to hear it.

"So…still don't want any help?"

I crank my neck with what little strength I have left, and I see the Sergeant taking a knee to reach down to my level. It reminds me of every time I dropped to the ground doing some kind of insane workout drill for him. In those days, I'd collapse on my stomach, and he'd bend down and shoot me that smug look of his, asking if I wanted to quit. I never quit, and I wasn't about to start now.

This time, however, he doesn't ask if I want to quit or chastise me in the slightest. Instead, he reaches his hand out to help lift me up. I don't take it, and not out of some kind of egotistical proof of my strength, but because I can't move my arm enough to accept his help.

"I'm fine...I...I just need a moment," I stammer. This isn't a complete lie; even in the short time since I awoke, I can feel my body starting to return to normal. Normal enough to walk, at least.

I manage to get to one knee, which is strenuous enough. Once I rise to my feet, the Sergeant looks me straight in the eye and says, "Congratulations. You did it. I don't know how you managed to pull it off. But I'm proud of you."

# *EPILOUGE*

AFTER MY SEEMINGLY NEVER-ENDING BATTLE against the Uuziks, I can finally take a few days to rest and recover.

With RG-87 safe, the Federation managed to arrest any surviving Uuziks and do a full scan of the base, trying to dig up as much information as they could.

Meanwhile, I've been kept in Federation care for 48 hours to examine any lingering effects. Taking such a heavy dose of Calax Crystal liquid into my body has to be dangerous, but nothing seems to come of it. At least that anyone can spot yet.

Since the mission is complete, the Federation and I decide to go our separate ways. They want to hold a more formal ceremony and reward me for my work in saving the galaxy, but I decide to skip out. Not that anyone, least of all the Sergeant, is surprised. Big ceremonies with a bunch of annoying people in stuffy suits is the last place I want to be, and he and I be both know that. Instead, I take the payout for my work, and we agree to strike my battle against the Uuziks from the record books.

Of course, I hate to pass up a good amount of fame. But, on the other hand I was also trafficking Calax Crystals for the Bacardi, which under normal circumstances would land me in prison on some kind of far-off planet. Instead, we manage to reach an agreement. The only caveat is that I'm not allowed to bring any other crystals from RG-87 to the Bacardi, or I'll risk paying the price.

And even if I wanted to go back to that hellhole of a planet, now it's under Federation watch, which would make scavenging Calax Crystals next to impossible.

So, I take my money and leave without complaint. It'll be more than enough to buy a new ship, which I do right away. After all, I have to make a stop to inform the Bacardi of our unfortunate news.

Ready and with a new ship, although not quite up to my standards, I'm ready to make my long trip back to EL–11, where I'll be able to get a proper vessel. I've informed the president of the Bacardi about the situation, and although they're less than thrilled at the idea of not getting their Calax Crystals, for all the hell it cost me, I could care less. Besides, when I mention being on a Federation ship and that I could have them at the planet's proverbial doorstep by dinner, we manage to see eye to eye. Neither of us wish to get the Federation involved.

The trip back to EL-11 will take approximately 20 hours with the speed of my new, low-budget ship. But it'll give me some much-needed rest.

Sitting back in my cockpit, I set course and kick up my

feet, leaning back as I hurl through space, waiting for my next adventure to call. What it'll be, nobody can say. Certainly not me. But one thing is always certain: I'll be ready for it.

This is Rimor Dynex, signing off.

# AFTERWORD

Hello, and thank you for reading *Tales from a Mercenary in Space*. If you have read any of my books from the Elements Series, then you know I like to take a moment at the end to say thank you and talk about the book.

This has been quite the year. I've really tried to push myself, and work to create a brand. I made my own website, came up with branding styles and guidelines, a logo, and much more. It's been great to align everything I've been doing, and hopefully in the future, people will see my brand and recognize what it stands for right away!

As well, this was quite a different style book for me, but I really enjoyed it. Perhaps there will be more first person books in the future. Also, the concept of space is often a topic of books, and now I can see why. It's a massive universe out there, and you have so much freedom to explore creativity in whatever way you see fit. I was also curious to try and write a character who was accomplished, confident, crafty, and even cocky, while still making him human and vulnerable in moments. Hopefully you enjoyed the story!

The first thank you always goes to Stalking P, for her continued commitment to working with me, always being a pleasure to bounce ideas off of, and craft each character with such attention and care.

Second, my Editor Rob Peace. This is my first time working with him as an editor, but I am sure it won't be my last. He treated my story with great care, fixing more issues than I can count. I do sincerely apologize for my lack of grammar! So big thank you for your work and I promise to use more commas!

Of course, to my friends and family, thank you for working to keep my sanity, as I question everything I do in life. So, with that, I will say thank you once again for the support, and I hope you will join me for whatever the future holds.

# PLEASE REVIEW

If you enjoyed this book, please consider writing a review on Amazon.com or Kobo.com, Goodreads, or anywhere else. It really helps!